THE FAITHFUL TRAITOR

First Published in Great Britain 2026 by Mirador Publishing

Copyright © 2026 by John Adamson
Artwork Copyright © 2026 by Lucy Christian

All rights reserved. No part of this publication may be reproduced or transmitted, in any form or by any means, without permission of the publishers or author. Excepting brief quotes used in reviews.

First edition: 2026

Any reference to real names and places is purely fictional and are constructs of the author. Any offence the references produce is unintentional and in no way reflects the reality of any locations or people involved.

ISBN: 978-1-917411-53-0

Copyright Information
THE HOLY BIBLE, NEW INTERNATIONAL VERSION®, NIV® Copyright © 1973, 1978, 1984, 2011 by Biblica, Inc.® Used by permission. All rights reserved worldwide.

The Faithful Traitor

John Adamson

ALSO BY THE AUTHOR

THE INFORMANT
THE INSIDER
THE DECEIVER
MEN OF STRAW

Dedication

For Steve and Rachel, with much love.

PREFACE

In the thirty-eighth year of Asa king of Judah, Ahab son of Omri became king of Israel, and he reigned in Samaria over Israel twenty-two years. Ahab son of Omri did more evil in the eyes of the Lord than any of those before him. He not only considered it trivial to commit the sins of Jeroboam son of Nebat, but he also married Jezebel daughter of Ethbaal king of the Sidonians, and began to serve Baal and worship him. He set up an altar for Baal in the temple of Baal that he built in Samaria. Ahab also made an Asherah pole and did more to arouse the anger of the Lord, the God of Israel, than did all the kings of Israel before him.

1 Kings 16 v 29-33 (NIV)

1

BLADE

A soft knock awoke me partially from my deeper-than-planned snooze in my favourite chair. A woman, a miniature carved bull in the palm of her outstretched hand, entered without waiting and silently closed the door. I opened my mouth to speak but she put her finger to her lips and smiled. I could almost smell the wickedness which emanated from her every movement. My limbs were shaking with fear.

She placed the tiny bull on my table, its eyes turned in my direction. She bowed reverentially to the carving, then picked it up again with her left hand.

She pointed at me with her other hand, her fingers gesturing to me to do likewise. I felt haplessly entranced, knowing I was about to do whatever she wanted, inexorably drawn towards the idol. She knew she had me under her spell.

I shook my head at her in a pathetic attempt to protest. She put the wooden creature down and went to her pocket, eyes on fire with evil. I caught the glint of a blade, rising from her clenched fist. Her facial muscles tightened, and her chin and eyebrows rose as the knife reached the apex of its ascent. She shrieked wildly twice, then plunged the weapon towards my heart.

I sat bolt upright to find my shirt soaked in sweat. I needn't have panicked. The woman was gone.

As you may have guessed, the whole thing was a daytime nightmare, but one which recurred more frequently when I was in my bed. It was fledged from bitter experience and fearful imagination, to fly at will, it seemed, through any and many of my sleeping hours.

It wasn't the only one, either, but decency forbids my relating some of the others. Suffice it to say that this woman was not constrained by any sense of propriety or righteous behaviour.

Why should she have haunted me so? I knew not. Truth was, Jezebel had never been near me, partly as I wasn't a good looker as a young man. Others were not so lucky.

The bull? A symbol of her favourite god, Baal, who, amongst other guidance offered to his all too willing but deluded followers, promoted pleasure through sexual immorality and power. The bull was chosen to add a dimension of superhuman strength.

The nightmare always left me shaken, my sleep disturbed for hours, mentally going over my life's old ground looking for guilt. And I found it afresh on each occasion. I'm old now, but as my mind replays scenes from my life, I reproach myself for every past error or omission from those twistedly vivid memories of the decades now gone. Could I, could we, have stopped her?

I'm spending my failing years alone these days, in a

settlement some thirty minutes from Samaria. The city was built by royalty, who continue to own it. King Omri had done most of the work, but it was his son Ahab who had customised it to suit his wife Jezebel's proclivity for Baal and Asherah.

I cut a solitary figure in the village I now know as home. My family, friends and associates had failed me back in my birth town, Jezreel. Exile? Yes. Self-imposed banishment, absolutely. I know I had been right to choose this lonely path. With the exception of my grandfather and to some degree, my mother, my family turned into traitors. They shifted away from the Lord, accepting the culture of the unspeakable Queen Jezebel and the gutless Ahab and all his legendary wickedness. They were guilty of tolerating or even promoting that pair's abhorrent ways.

Samaria city wasn't for me. The palace there was a sight to behold with its prominent and decorative ivory, but I could not countenance seeing it. Nor could I be a tenant of either Ahab or Jezebel, after the destruction they wrought back in Jezreel where they lived before the new residence was made ready for them and their disgusting ways.

Am I bitter? Yes. I have every right to be. My anger burns against the Lord for not protecting me and those once dear to me when I needed Him to. When I left Jezreel that final time, it was to see out my days in the righteous knowledge that I had done no wrong. Jezreel and those who blighted my existence there are now but a distant memory.

And yet those nightmares bug me. My old grandad, whom I loved, told me that God communicates through dreams, but why would He bother with me? I'm not like the rest of them.

I've been on His side since my childhood ended. I am a faithful. And what's more, I had determined that nothing was ever going to change me now.
Or so I thought.

2

YESH

Halfway through one unremarkable morning recently, there was a knock on the door. I checked before opening it, to be greeted by the figure of what looked like a traveller. Before I could tell him to clear off, he seized my hands warmly and smiled broadly.

"You're a hard man to find, Eran! This place is quite remote. Remember me?"

What ensued turned the day distinctly remarkable. The man knew my name. I looked hard at the grey-haired figure who stood before me, slightly bent over his walking stick. There was something about him, maybe his eyes, which recalled the early days with Sharon, my older sister, Dad and Mum and my paternal grandad, in Jezreel. But could that be true? Really?

He spotted that I was flummoxed and squeezed my fingers reassuringly, like my mum used to do when I was a youngster.

"It's been a long time, Eran. A very long time. We were kids together in Jezreel."

"Erm, you can't be Joel, then. Those were teenage times." Then it came to me. Those eyes? It could only be my best friend from when I was five years old. I wished he hadn't come, but it was too late. "Yesh?"

"That's me. You and Sharon played with me. She was a bit of a tomboy, I recall. Remember those spy games? You always wanted to be the secret agent, making me the villain."

"Sharon was your evil sidekick, whatever the context. Happy days indeed, Yesh."

"Indeed, Eran. You always played the secret agent. Sharon was a good sport. My mum and yours were friends. We played together as kids, families together, but it all went pear shaped when that dreadful King Omri died."

He came into the house, of course. Yesh had a warmth about him which I couldn't define, but he was from the happiest times of my life.

I went with the cautious option. "It's longer than I care to remember, Yesh. Decades. Listen, you didn't find me by chance, did you? Someone has put you up to this. Jezreel is a long way from here."

He indicated that we should sit down. First, I found some food and water to offer him, then did as he had bid.

"Eran, I'm of an age when you look back at your life, and I remembered your name."

I wasn't buying that line. "I wasn't born yesterday, mate."

"Precisely. Neither of us were. That's why I'm here."

"So why you, Yesh? Why now? Why at all?"

"Ok, Eran, I owe you an explanation. It's been a momentous time in Jezreel for ages, of course, but never more so than over the last few days. You'll have heard the news."

"I don't do current affairs, Yesh. No-one does in this place."

"Shall I update you?"

"If you must. But first tell me why you are here. And not because we weren't born yesterday."

He took that as an attempt at humour. It wasn't, but it didn't matter. His response sounded slightly hollow anyway. "Ho, ho! We laughed a lot when we were little."

We did, I think. Despite myself, were my frosty edges beginning to melt? I found myself trying to smile.

He went on. "Eran, there's some bad news. Remember Elijah's lieutenant, old Obadiah? He passed away shortly before I set off to find you. I was at the interment, my friend. Some of the top people were there. When it came to the eulogy, his importance in supporting Elijah became apparent. There were so many gaps in his story, though. Just before he died, he mentioned your family, so here I am."

The news didn't shock me, but Yesh's story was almost credible. "I had some dealings with the man. He was a man of the Lord, a faithful, so I have respect for him. Why can't he just be left in peace?"

"He was more than just a man of God, Eran. Look, our nation needs as complete a record of his life and times as we can find. One of the musicians at the service also told me that you would have information, and that you were last reported living somewhere in Samaria. I told them of our shared childhood, and all things considered, they decided I was a shoo-in as their emissary."

I was being drawn in. "I'm not going back there, Yesh. If you think you've come to fetch me home in some way, you can forget it. I've got too many bad memories of Jezreel. Anyway, it's a very long walk. I don't even contemplate it these days."

"Me neither. I'll be frank, option one was my bringing you

back. Let's go with option two. Can you put me up for a day or two? If you won't come back, then I need to hear your memories here. All of them. In full."

I bought a moment or two with a diversion. "How did you get here, Yesh, if you didn't plod through the sand?"

"Ah, they provided me with a camel and an escort. I still found it tiring. When we got to Samaria, we still had to find you in a limited time. The camel's due back in Jezreel before too long." He had spotted my delaying ploy and reverted to his initial request. "Will you tell me your story?"

The heat was on, climate-wise and personally. I tried another delaying tactic, offered him a nap. After all, he was exhausted after his journey.

He didn't fall for it. "Willingly, if you give me your word about recounting your recollections."

I had a shot at damage limitation. "Just about Obadiah?"

Yesh was a sharp cookie. "Ah, no. His demise comes at the end of a whole era of trauma, probably the worst of our whole history as God's people. We need everything. Others are doing it too, if that helps."

I began to feel flattered. Was he giving me the full picture? Possibly. I decided that I would do it, but it would be warts and all. I gathered my thoughts as well as some supplies when Yesh dozed. The times when, but also after we'd been kids together, the breakdown of my family relationships, the suffering, the hunger, the blessings, the brighter days, it all flooded back, but mostly, I recalled having so many unanswered questions. Oh, and memories of Obadiah, and therefore Elijah, of course. Both had a lot to do with it, but Obadiah was going to be my specialist subject.

Yesh awoke an hour later and returned cheerfully, only to find that my more positive mindset had lost a little intensity. I'd had too much time to mull it all over, I fear, and that nightmare syndrome still had its effect. I had to confront him with my concerns.

"Yesh, Can I check something which doesn't add up for me? Why would my wretched family be of interest to anyone recording the history of these last years? Obadiah was a faithful. They weren't. Some were traitors. Me? I was like the scapegoat, sent into the desert to separate them from their misdeeds and bring them a false sense of forgiveness. There was only my grandfather who stood by his beliefs. Yesh, I suspect there's a hidden agenda in your visit, and I need to know what it is."

He didn't flinch, to be fair. "It's not hidden, Eran, it's just complex. There are many reasons which have come together recently to bring me here now. I haven't told you everything yet. I will, but it will only make sense in the context of events. Shall we start with a very significant recent happening?"

He sounded genuine. "Go on, Yesh."

"Obadiah died shortly before another noteworthy death in Jezreel. I can tell you, my friend, that matters concerning Jezebel and King Ahaziah, have moved on dramatically. Ahaziah was killed in battle. Great changes may be coming, Eran. The king has gone."

"And Jezebel? Our very dear queen?"

"I'll save that story till we've caught up. It's a big one. Look, Eran, your family was so closely linked to the palace in Jezreel. We need your witnessing over Ahaziah's reign here."

I went cold. This was huge. He didn't need to remind me

that Jezebel and her evil hubby were once in our hometown until the seat of power was moved to Samaria after a previous significant royal death. That was when the southern kingdom was under its own monarch and ruled from Jerusalem. Why was that? A tribal dispute split our people, with ten choosing to rule the north and two, those of Benjamin and Judah, taking the south.

Neither kingdom was perfect, of course, like me, but our lot probably strayed much further from the Lord. Was the same Lord requiring me to have a part in holding Jezebel to account in front of my nation? It was a weighty burden if so.

Yesh gave me a moment for my thoughts. He was intuitive. "Your mum was called Ayala, right?"

I nodded. "And Dad was called Manny. He let me down badly. Because of him, I decided never to marry. If it just brought strife, as he did, I'd prefer to be on my own."

Yesh smiled calmly. I didn't tell him that weirdly, I missed being part of the family, dwindling as it was. I felt conflicted. With me as a confirmed bachelor, would a new generation ever happen? Sharon's experience of Dad was almost as bad as mine. I couldn't see marriage and kids appealing to her either.

Yesh read me. He put his hand on mine. "Shall we talk family before we talk Jezebel?"

I found myself squeezing his fingers. He'd won. "Yes, let's do that."

"Yes. Maybe you tell me your story, Eran. Let me decide if you need to come home to Jezreel."

"I can't promise that, Yesh, but I will accept your first request." I still wasn't being tricked that easily.

I explained that Dad was a lost cause. For the key years of our story, he was a traitor, switching to Jezebel's agenda. That hostility left its mark indelibly on our relationship, and that with Sharon too. He had drifted beyond the love he showed by the shed load during our early years into this brute of a man during our adolescence, and it all began with a trip to the palace.

Mum's knack for finding the right balance between encouragement, correction and empathy during teenage years into adulthood came right back into my head. For the first time in so many years, I missed her. Slightly emotionally, I told him that it was her I needed now, not Dad.

I gulped. "So, any news of Mum, Yesh?" I was curious about my father but couldn't bring myself to ask. It was as if I wanted to find he was dead.

"Oh. You didn't hear?"

I pre-empted his next statement. "They're both gone, aren't they?"

"I'm afraid so. A couple of years back."

He paused to see if I reacted. Externally, I don't think I did.

"There's something I have to tell you there, but we'll leave that for now, Eran."

I was not in the mood for niceties. "Erm, there's still Sharon, Yesh. I don't have a clue what happened to her, as we fell out so badly after I found she wasn't a faithful."

"Sharon? Your sister? She's been hard to locate since recent happenings. Keeping a low profile. I didn't have time to search."

I stayed cool. "She became close to Jezebel, Yesh. Was she still working for her?"

"Yes, Eran, very much so. Where Jezebel went, so did Sharon. Ot at least she used to. But let's go back to the beginning."

I agreed. Was it that I'd revisited these scenes so many times, obsessively searching for my own guilt, or was I being filled with the Lord's blessing? They say He's the Lord of the Ages, so maybe. Either way, I was transported back to those early days in Jezreel. I was taking Yesh back in time with me to picture it, starting in our family home. Yesh indicated to me that he was ready.

In my mind, I was back there as a kid, playing at espionage with him and Sharon, with Mum watching over us. Joy filled my heart, so much that I barely heard his next words.

He knew. He nudged me gently forward in time. "I loved those days, Eran. Now take me to after we'd lost touch, my friend. Start me with a scene in your family home when you were a teen."

Was the Lord inspiring me? The elation I was feeling was not an emotion I had experienced, maybe ever, and my experiences felt like an all-encompassing drama. A fierce desire overcame me, demanding that I tell the story as it was being re-lived in my mind, and not from a dry historical perspective.

I had been transformed into that teen again, starting out on I knew not what. And what a journey it was to become. It started one day in our family home, at the end of the working day.

3

SADDLE

My dad wiped his hands and nodded in my direction. "That was some shift today, Son. Hard graft."

Dad's full name was Emmanuel, but Mum only ever called him Manny. My elder sister Sharon, sometimes known as Shaz, was our own recently appointed royal beautician. Mum was Ayala. She got called Ay, which was confusing during the harvest, and that's when you find us today.

I sniffed. "It would be easier if you weren't so bossy, Dad. You didn't used to be." He was regularly on my case, my dad, since a few weeks beforehand. Grandad completed the family residential set-up and regularly spoke up for me. He was a total star, and I could express my feelings more strongly when he was around, because he'd always got my back.

Dad knows how I feel about Grandad. "I've got to be tough at harvest, Eran. Especially when it's as good as this one."

I couldn't resist the bait and winked surreptitiously at Grandad. "Life's not just about work, except in this family."

Dad looked at his father. "He wouldn't be saying that if there was no bread on the table, eh, Grandad?"

Grandad pointed at me. "Don't knock the lad, Manny. He's a good 'un. And he's right, in a way."

Dad was being drawn in. I grinned inwardly as he started on Grandad. Foolishly, of course. Grandad could look after himself verbally. But Dad couldn't stop himself. "Right? What do you mean, right? He's a kid. What would he know?"

Grandad grinned outwardly. He knew when to pull back. "Okay, he needs to learn, I'll give you that."

Dad sensed his opportunity to mount his usual high horse. "Learn to graft, that's what. That's proper education. Like I do. Keeping my family in a decent house with good food to eat."

Did he graft? He did when he was there. Yet it didn't stop him taking time out. He had recently found a regular business meeting, as he called it, to attend. It always left me to add his labouring workload to my own.

Grandad's look confirmed to me that I shouldn't chirp up. It was left to Mum to encourage Dad down from his mount. "Come on boys, dinner's ready. Let's keep it civilised. Eran, give Sharon a shout, will you? She's had a hard day at the palace."

I knew what was coming next and I wasn't having it. Getting at me was one thing, but his aim was shifting to my sister. I made my point. "I will, but she can do without Dad turning on her during the meal. He's been coming across as very harsh on Shaz, of late, like he is with me."

Mum's voice suggested a measure of insistence. "He doesn't mean it, Son. He's trying to be funny. Lighten things up. Isn't that right, Manny?"

Dad shuffled on his metaphorical saddle then remained

firmly ensconced. His next contribution made it clear that he wasn't planning to descend any time soon. "Eran, go and get Queen Sharon. She'll be in her bedroom, fixing her make-up."

"You're at it already, Dad. You don't even know what Shaz is doing."

Mum rolled her eyes and motioned me to go. He hadn't finished. "Don't tell me she works hard. She's pampered. Indoors all day, serving the king's family with a bunch of other beauticians. It's not proper graft. I sometimes wonder why I got her in there, given the amount of use she is."

This was what Shaz had to deal with. I paused at the doorway to fire a timely reminder at him. "Dad, you told us what an honour it was when she was taken on. She sometimes works with Queen Jezebel. That's no easy task."

"That's different. A fine woman, our queen, Eran. Mark my words, she's a lady with a clear vision. She has to look the part. Helping her to do so when there's ten others to do the same job has got to be a cushy number. How can that be tough?"

"Have you ever bothered asking her, Dad?"

Dad hadn't. I knew that, but he told us anyway. "No. It's obvious. By the way, what's that racket from across the street?"

Mum spotted another chance to bring some peace. "That's the new neighbour's boy. He's a musician. He plays a stringed instrument. Maybe the harp."

I didn't miss my chance. "Lyre."

Mum grinned. Dad wasn't for laughing. "A musician? How useful! Another waste of space. What's his name?"

Mum kept trying as Sharon entered the room. "Joel, I believe. Nice boy."

I tried to help, mostly because I was starving. "Shall we move to the table, Mum?"

Mum's eyes were for Shaz. "You look lovely, darling. Will you give thanks for us, Eran? That would also be lovely."

Dad's mood had still not lifted. "Who's he giving thanks to? It should be to me."

Mum smiled weakly. "Erm, the Lord, isn't it?"

Dad returned the facial expression. "Not necessarily. Nobody prays to him these days. If you don't keep up with the times, Ayala, you won't ever understand your kids. Trust me."

Mum exhaled. "Sorry Manny, I do my best."

I sensed Dad was coming off his steed at last, and he gradually calmed down.

I wasn't the only one to spot that. Grandad raised his hand. "I'm giving thanks to the Lord like my own father taught me. Silently if I need to. That's what we should all do."

Dad differed. No surprise there lately, even though his tone was less bombastic. Not sure why, but he never used to be like this. "Tradition without questioning is a hollow, meaningless gesture, Father. I've not seen much evidence of any god giving me a hand on the farm, although Baal seems more relevant to the growing process."

"Baal?" Grandad paused for effect. "Forgive the agricultural pun, but you are forgetting your roots, my son."

"Look, everyone's doing it. Pick the god who can help you with what you want, or if you prefer, don't even bother. Just work harder. Baal's the one for me."

Grandad tutted. "No wonder your kids are confused. You're building on sand, Manny. The shifting sands of contemporary culture."

Mum changed the subject. "Come on, let's lighten up. Sharon, how was your day really?"

"Mum, the queen spent some time with us today. She's incredibly beautiful. She's got a figure to die for."

"I hope you bowed, Sharon."

"Oh yes, we all did. They say you don't want to get on the wrong side of her or you're out."

Dad couldn't keep his mouth shut. In terms of his lanky equine, I thought he was stretching a foot towards the stirrup for a full remount. "She obviously knows her mind, as I was saying. That's good. Royalty needs focussed policies and the drive to achieve targets. The king made a good choice when he married her. You'd better be careful. I moved heaven and earth to persuade Obadiah to get you that job."

Shaz grimaced. "Dad, Queen Jezebel may be very pretty, but she scares me. There's something I don't like in the way she stares at us. Something's going on. Listen, I'm giving the job a chance, but if it doesn't improve, I might be handing in my notice."

Dad sighed. His shoulders dropped, signalling the end of the rant and the reluctant abandonment of that high horse. "Obeying orders is never easy, Sharon. Humans aren't made to just accept instructions without question. Get used to it."

I looked at him pointedly, then moved my gaze to my sister. "Shaz, does that remind you of someone?"

He didn't take the bait. Shaz flashed a smile at me but had more to say. "It's not that, Dad. The others feel the same. What's going on is in her head, like, mental. She's not like how you portray her, you know, rational and measured. Jezebel is weird."

Dad emitted a low whistle. "Don't ever tell her that, Sharon, or you won't need to hand any notice in for your employment. Don't put your neck on the line or there'll be a noose round it. Just do your job and come home to relax."

Did I see him wink at her? Anyway, I couldn't stop myself. "Relax? Are you planning to be out in the evenings then, Dad? She can't relax with you in the room!"

He'd heard enough. "Don't you be so cheeky, Son. Now shut up and eat your dinner, both of you."

4

WAILING

We did shut up and eat, subdued by an unspoken truce. Grandad understood how we were feeling. "Listen, you two, why don't we have a short walk after dinner? I can't manage too far these days, but some fresh air would be nice. What do you say?"

Sharon was first to respond. "Count me in, Grandad. I love spending time with you."

I followed suit but heard a hint of my father's dog-with-a-bone obstinacy in my own words. "Me too. And I hope that the music is still playing from the neighbours' property. I find it compelling."

He couldn't let that go, of course. "Do what you want, but this is my house, and my rules are what count. Don't you forget that. And while you're out, tell that lad to keep the noise down. We all need a bit of peace without him wailing away."

This was a war I couldn't win, so I turned to my sister and tried a tangential but beautifully annoying tactic to succeed in today's verbal battle. "Sharon, was there music in the palace today?"

She seemed to know what I was doing and replied enthusiastically. "Yes. The queen just claps her hands twice and they play. When she wants them to stop, she does the same thing three times."

I couldn't help grinning. "How lovely! Music all day if you want it. Is she into modern?"

Dad fixed her with a controlling stare, so she retreated to uncontroversial issues. "Dunno. It's just boring old stuff they play. I talked to one of the musicians today and he claimed they just fear making mistakes. One of them did yesterday and wasn't there today."

"And do they know what happened to him?"

"No. Not a word. No-one dared ask. Probably the end of his palace career, at least, if you ask me."

Dad was back in the conversation. "The queen knows how to stop musicians in full flow. I admire that. Why? Because they don't do anything useful. Not like farmhands."

Dinner was done, Grandad was ready, so we gathered by the front door. Grandad's tone was warm and friendly. "Now then, you pair, let's talk. But not till we've said hello to our young musician. Music is made to be enjoyed."

Sharon relaxed. "Okay Grandad. Then there's things I want to ask. You and Eran do the talking. I'm shy at times like this."

I was so proud of Grandad's opening words when he approached our neighbour. "Lovely music, young man. How did you learn to play and sing like that?"

The respect was shared. "Good evening, Sir. I am learning under a brilliant young musician called Elijah."

Grandad affected amazement. "The Elijah? The one who writes songs to the Lord?"

"That's the one. He's training us to teach people about Him through songs. I'm working on one called 'Your Way Yahweh' right now."

Grandad shook his hand. "Sounds good! Great name! Do all your songs have catchy titles?"

"No Sir, I'm learning about naming songs. It's very important. This one was provided for all of us by Elijah. He speaks of inspiration being the principal key to good songwriting."

"I've heard so much about Elijah. He's quite moody, isn't he? Most creative artists are. May I ask your name?"

The young man hesitated a moment. "Erm, Joel, Sir. And Elijah's usually okay with us."

Grandad wanted to know more. "Would you describe him as vivacious?"

Joel shook his head and grinned. "I wouldn't dare call him that, Sir. What you see…."

Grandad finished the expression. "…is what you get. Right?"

Joel's face changed. "Not exactly, Sir. I was going to say is a man whom the Lord holds close. He has a spirit which seems to come directly from God."

Grandad put him at his ease. "I'm impressed you could see that."

We knew that, for sure, but Grandad used the compliment to draw him in. Smart, I thought, then decided to join the conversation. "And I'm Eran, and this is my sister Sharon. Hi. We love music. We're into modern. My sister's very shy. Especially when she sees someone she might like."

Grandad pulled a face and winked at the blushing figure of

Sharon. "Eran, give over. I know you're joking, but there's a time and a place."

I regretted my comment immediately and could only apologise. "And this is not it. Sorry."

Joel shook his head nonchalantly before adding a reassuring dash of charm. "Listen, it's good to meet you both. And is this your father, Sharon?"

Sharon didn't engage as her anxiety got the better of her. "Erm, erm, no. He's my grandad." She looked away.

The last-named re-took centre stage. "Joel, I like you already! I have the privilege of being grandfather to both these two fine young people. Sharon works at the palace and Eran labours for his father, Manny. He's a farmer."

I found Joel's warmth increasingly compelling. "Are there plenty of others like you who are training to make music for a living, Joel?"

Joel shrugged before smiling at Sharon. "Fewer, these days. Our songs are not as fashionable as they were a few years ago. There's less and less demand. People don't seem to feel they need that kind of teaching in recent times. But we do more than sing. Elijah teaches us to speak about the Lord too."

My sister was encouraged. Joel's smile had not been wasted. She made eye contact. "Will you need to think again about your career, Joel? I'm sure you're going to be great at what you do."

Joel acknowledged the question. "Probably, Sharon. In recent times, we've had to learn some secular music for the palace at the queen's request. Elijah won't touch that, but we have to do it. But listen, I must get on. New material to work on. Enjoy your walk."

Grandad nodded. "Go well, Joel. Go well."

5

PATIENCE

With that, the young musician withdrew inside his house, and we strolled on our way. Sharon's expression was puzzled. I wondered if it was to do with Joel, but then I remembered her words just prior to meeting him. "Grandad, is Dad right about other gods?"

He stroked his chin. "Being the head of the family is never easy, Sharon. A dad has to work hard to keep everyone together, and that's never simple."

"That wasn't my question."

He opened his palms towards her. "Patience, my dear, patience. It's a long game."

Her perplexed look moved through bewilderment to acceptance. I felt the urge to help her by changing the topic. "Grandad, do you remember the last king?"

He seemed pleased to be asked. "Who could forget him? King Omri. His reign was not one to be celebrated, Eran."

"Why not?" Shaz beat me to the question.

"Sharon, when a king dies, people look back over the lifetime achievements he has made. His were dire. He had learned nothing from previous monarchs and didn't seem to care."

"So, what about King Ahab now? What do you make of him?"

Grandad motioned us to move close to him. "Never ask that question in public, you two. Never." His voice turned to barely a whisper. "Let's just say, like father, like son."

My shade of pale was mirrored on my sister's face. Grandad noticed, of course, and smiled. The whispering was over, and our little huddle finished with it.

Grandad's voice was back to normal. "You'll be fine. Your dad was invited to a meeting at the palace a few months back, and he met the king and the queen. That's when he got you the job there, Sharon. If you keep on the right side of them, you'll flourish. You won't get hurt."

I knew he was choosing his words. I couldn't help but feel there was some hollowness there, maybe because we were out in public, and resolved to talk some more with him when the opportunity arose.

There was a trace of our father's obstinacy in Shaz which I hadn't observed before, although she did it with far more sensitivity. She returned to the burning question which Grandad thought he had neatly parked. "So is Dad right about the Lord?"

He muffled a sigh before taking a moment. "Okay, Sharon. You do know that every generation thinks they know more than the one before, don't you?"

I knew he was addressing me too. Shaz still looked puzzled, so he went on. "Thinking that way is an age-old mistake, believe me. It's human nature to want to believe that. Let me tell you something very important."

If Grandad stated that it was significant, it was exactly so. We were both all ears.

"Don't look to humans for the source of wisdom. Wisdom is found in the divine, in the Lord. He remains the same across time, across every generation. The way we live and what we think as humans may change, but He doesn't."

I sensed where he was heading. This was a message about our dad. My next careless question caused more concern than I'd bargained for.

"So, Grandad, you think things have started to go wrong?"

He looked around and called us close again. "You can't talk like that. It's not wise." He checked the surroundings again. "Wrong? Yes. The Lord is our God, and we are His people. There is no other god out there. Just the one. And our king and queen would do well to heed that."

Shaz wasn't sure. Her voice was hardly audible. "But other nations don't agree, Grandad. Are they wrong too?"

"I know that, and it's tough. If you are brought up to believe in something else, or in a particular way of doing things, it's really hard. But, Sharon, the truth, pure and simple, has to be our guide."

"Why's that? Can't their god be another way of understanding the same life we all share?" Shaz was back to normal volume. Grandad's alarm showed in his eyes and she mouthed an apology before continuing softly. "Like Baal, or Asherah? Why does it have to be so difficult?"

Grandad nodded. "It doesn't. We want to accept people from other cultures, and we want to accommodate them among us, sure, and that's good. But truth is truth. It's an absolute. It's non-negotiable."

My sister tilted her head slightly. "I just don't want to upset anyone's feelings. I see that happening to others all the time with my dad, and I know how it feels to be the victim."

Grandad's arm went around her shoulder. "Love, I've seen more years than you. Trust me, hold to truth. For now, why don't you both listen to Joel when he's singing songs to the Lord? That young man has the Lord's truth at the heart of his music, with the power to touch and move you."

"Is that how I should cope with Dad?" Was there a hint of hollowness in her question? I didn't know. Then her eyes opened wide, anticipating the reply.

Grandad smiled. "I think so. Connect with the Lord, both of you. Especially you Sharon, right now. Joel's songs will lift you beyond what you tolerate at work. Listen to him when he plays his racket, as your dad calls it, and you'll find yourself wanting more. You won't be clapping your hands three times to stop it like Jezebel; you'll be dancing for joy."

Grandad seemed to have proved me right in one thing, for sure. "I'm grateful that you know there's more to this life than work, Grandad. And I promise we will both think about your words."

His expression became serious. "We live in troubled times, you two. Always remember where you are, and to whom you are talking. Stay safe."

6

ROCK

For a teenager, I thought long and hard about Grandad's words. A good two minutes. I jest; it was much more than that. Shaz didn't talk to me about what he'd told us, but that was the way we rubbed along.

Grandad spotted us as he was leaving the house a couple of days later and called us both to come outside the front door. I thought that was so my mum and dad wouldn't hear, so was keen to listen. It was brief.

I wasn't the only one who'd been reflecting. His voice was confidential and his words rather mysterious. "Eran, Sharon, when you are a little older, you will better understand the Lord's truth and see your shared duty as His people. It is not to compromise, to accommodate, to water down, but to build our nation back into His love and protection."

Shaz shook her head. "How will we know when that time comes, Grandad?"

"The Lord will tell you. Stay close to Him. For now, you must exercise extreme caution. Whatever happens, don't do anything dramatic."

I wasn't exactly planning to start a missionary movement at that point, and neither was my sis, but we were both engaged by his demeanour and went along with his drift.

Shaz screwed up her nose. "Cautious? Dramatic? Why so? The Lord is simply good news, isn't He?"

Grandad shook his head. "That's not what I mean, Sharon. There are forces around us which seek to destroy those who know the truth." He stared at her. "To kill them."

I couldn't help myself. "Is this the danger you told us about, Grandad?"

Grandad permitted himself a smile. He spoke firmly, with commitment. "Remember to seek the protection of the Lord. He stands firm, like a rock. The winds don't blow Him anywhere. He wins, my dears. We do too, at the end of life's chase."

With that, he left us standing there and headed to the city. Did I see a neighbour's face disappearing at a door a few yards away? Had he been overheard?

Shaz had seen the apparition too. She exhaled. "What was that about?"

I stepped onto the street to make certain no-one was listening before responding. The face had gone. "Not sure. But Grandad's definitely not on the same part of the scroll as Dad, Shaz."

Fifteen minutes later, Grandad reappeared on the horizon accompanied by a young man. As they approached, I realised it was Joel. They joined us.

Grandad's mood had changed. He grinned. "I was heading to the city square to stretch my old legs and to meet a few friends of mine when I met young Joel here. We got chatting, so I walked back with him. He didn't know my real name!"

Sharon was intrigued. "What did you tell him?"

"I told him that he could call me Grandad once he felt comfortable with the idea. I don't mind; I'm just flattered that he wants to talk to an old fella like me. It seems he had no teacher today, so he's come home."

Joel nodded. "Yes. Elijah wasn't there today. They reported that he'd gone on a mission."

Grandad looked at him approvingly. "That sounds good. He prophesies with great power for those who listen. Which town?"

"No, I mean he had a job to do. Other than training the likes of me. Obadiah called by to tell us we'd got a day off. All very sudden and hush hush, Sir."

I'd heard that Obadiah had a tough remit. He was a palace official, an administrator. He had appointed Elijah to the music role and was an ardent supporter of the prophet. He was a diplomat, skilled in the art of allowing other people to have his, and the Lord's, own way. He used his channels well in a position where his own faith was under threat.

But I digress. Back to the day off. I like a good mystery. "Ooh! Day off? I love a bit of intrigue! What's going on, Joel? Behind the scenes, I mean. Is it the king?"

"Ahab? Yes and no. Yes, he runs the whole show most of the time, but he seems to have a problem."

"So, what's rattled his sabre? What's his agenda?"

"Ahab's focus right now is solely to maintain the military prowess his father built up. Ten tribes, ten fine fighting units, that's all he cares about. Everything else is just left to tick along. He doesn't bother, so long as there's no trouble."

Grandad's expression altered. "Joel, be careful with what you say."

Joel raised a hand. "It's important we stick to our principles, Sir. I will speak out. You see, people don't always appreciate that Ahab has an open faith policy. He will let his people worship who they will. His father did that."

It was as I thought. "Is that a cause for fear, though? Really?"

Joel winced. "He speaks of freedom."

Grandad's intervention was swift, but quiet. "That's not freedom. Freedom is given by the Lord, not by the king. Be careful, Joel. It's not Ahab who is overseeing that policy, as you've just told us."

Joel's confidence was reflected in a drop in his tone. "Ok, it's the queen, I know. You're right. She's a bit unpredictable."

"Ahab isn't great news either, Joel. Open faith policy or not, he has been positively promoting other gods. His wife's view of freedom isn't the same as his own, I'm told."

Joel nodded. "That's what Elijah thinks too. Obadiah is a skilful communicator, but there's always been an underlying risk of a confrontation anytime soon. Jezebel might even take on Elijah, never mind Obadiah. It might even have just kicked off today. That might be why Elijah's not at work."

Grandad pursed his lips before speaking. "Elijah needs to be very circumspect. It could be foolish to directly confront the king or the queen. Saying that, Ahab should remember that although Jezebel may be queen, she's still his subject. He's the main man."

Joel opened up. "Yes, Sir. Obadiah has seen what's really

happening. Jezebel's got her own agenda. Of late, the king takes care of military matters and leaves the rest to the queen. She reports to him, of course, but when they disagree, he just gives in. She is a powerful woman. That's the threat to Elijah."

I intervened. "Oh dear. One flutter of her eyelashes and she gets what she's after, right?"

Sharon fixed me with a stare, but Joel had more to add. "It's worse than that. Elijah told Obadiah that she's iniquitous. He says it's like she's been taken over by an evil spirit and constantly exudes wickedness."

7

MOUTHPIECE

Grandad's jaw fell. "That's so not like Elijah. He's always been a positive influence since we've known him, seeking the best in everyone. Except when he's having a period of self-doubt, of course, but even those are rarer these days."

Joel agreed. "You know him well, I'd say."

"Me? Not really. For me, he's still relatively new on the block, but we talk about it in the city square. Call it collective wisdom."

"Well, Obadiah needs all his diplomatic skills to help Elijah seek the right moment. Telling Ahab and Jezebel to get rid of their false gods, Baal and Asherah, is not going to have them dancing for joy."

"Joel, is it me or could a spirit have got into Elijah? A good one, I mean. Is that why he's so much stronger than a year or two back?"

Shaz and I looked on nervously as Joel continued. "We'll only know when we see if he goes through with it, even when his timing is right. He's got to get through royal security first, remember."

Grandad emitted a low whistle. "Joel, will you report back to me when you know more? We need to stick together."

Joel understood. "Sure. I'll find you. Give me forty-eight hours."

I was putting in my usual farm shift when they met again. Two days had elapsed, as Joel had requested. That evening, Grandad took me aside. "I spoke to our young musician friend earlier."

"What did he have to say, Grandad?"

"Firstly, Eran, there's been neither sight nor sound of Elijah. The music department has been suspended."

"What do you mean, suspended? And where's he gone? Has he been taken?"

"Calm down, Eran. Joel informed me that Obadiah's on the case. I was relieved. Too much drama in one week is not good for me at my time of life."

"What had taken place, Grandad?"

"Elijah told Obadiah that something had cropped up."

"And what might that have been?"

"It was a voice in his head, Eran. Joel then told me what they'd been doing just before all this happened. They'd been working on songs praising the Lord for the harvest, drawing inspiration from the story of Moses."

"And then?"

"Well, it seems that Elijah got this word that there's going to be a famine. No precipitation, no moisture, for years to come."

"Here, Grandad? That's not great news, especially in our family. Do you think it was the Lord speaking?"

"It's not great news for anyone, Eran. The Lord? Yes,

Elijah pronounced himself sure of that. But there's more. He thinks that the Lord is using him as His mouthpiece. And, my boy, the famine will only end when the Lord prompts Elijah to call on the rain to fall."

"That's some claim. I'm out of my depth here. But isn't Elijah sticking his neck out with that one?"

"He is. That's why Obadiah thinks it's true, Eran. And Elijah may be doing that literally."

"Literally? Surely a decent king would be glad to hear him, do some advance planning and make provision."

"You'd think so but remember the king's not the major problem. It's his missus."

"Even with something as vital as this?"

"I'm afraid so. She doesn't believe the Lord actually exists. It appears that she didn't take the news of the famine seriously. She said if he's getting voices in his head, it's time he got help. And she would provide it."

"Was that a threat, Grandad?"

"Yes. Her style of help will be to put the offending body part on a plate. She needs to snuff out His message along with those who proclaim it."

"Did Joel relate what happened when Elijah told the king? Did he even know that? A power struggle?"

"He knew, yes. Queen J. was there too, pulling all the royal strings. But then Elijah heard another voice."

"I'm sure I'd have had one in my head telling me to get out of town. Did he?"

"Out of town, Eran? Spot on. Yes. And he's gone. But there was more. The voice told Elijah precisely where to head. A remote, safe place."

"Won't he starve if he goes remote?" My concern was genuine.

"The Lord told him there'd be water and food there."

"How was he sure that the voice was the Lord's? And didn't something similar happen to Moses?"

"Well remembered, young man! That's how Elijah is confident about who's speaking. It's authenticated by what you just recalled. He's sure it is the Lord at work."

"Wow, Grandad, that's quite something. What did Joel say?"

"He started talking about you and your sister. It seemed important to him."

"And?"

"He told me he liked you both and that he thinks Sharon is quite a looker!"

"And how did you respond, Grandad? About Shaz?"

"I told him I thought she's a good girl who knows a good cosmetic when she sees one! He agreed and told me Sharon was brave too. He admires her courage. He knows she's got a tough job. Then I came out with something surprising."

"And what was that, Grandad? Do tell!"

"Well, given what he's learning to do for a living, I told him that Sharon needs convicting."

"And?" I was hooked.

"Joel's face fell. He asked me what she had done wrong. I laughed, then reassured him that I meant convicting that the Lord is the one and only God. You do too, if I'm honest. You both might need more experience of life to work that out, but Joel's influence can only be good."

"Shaz and experience of life? She'll get that at the palace, for sure."

"Yes, she will. I told him that you two will value him as a friend. I told him to hang in there for you both."

"Thanks Grandad."

"He mentioned that you were a very decent lad too. Make sure you listen to him. Don't say anything, but he's not sure of your parents, though. He's rather wary, if I'm honest."

"Oh? Both of them?"

"Not totally. I told him your mum wavers a bit but she's usually fine. My take is that she doesn't like to cause controversy so has the odd wobble, but her heart is primarily with the Lord. Your dad is different. He's blowing like the barley in summer, this way and that. Sometimes he loses the plot."

"Does Joel know what Dad thinks of him?"

"He suspects, Eran. He's not sure your father thinks he's much use."

"You're not wrong, Grandad. He has little regard for musicians and, to me, even less for the Lord."

"What's Joel's own take on his career?"

"He made it clear that when he's asked what he does, he tells people that in his job he works to bring those who stray from the truth back to the right track. And he offered to put your father on his to-do list! My advice to him was that he was doing great work, but to remember that everything has its time. I told him that you believed that the Lord is King. Joel agreed, and added that God ruled over friendship, love and life, and that we all need to hold fast to His way."

8

Lipstick

Just then, we were interrupted. The approach of dinner time that evening did not need any gong or formal announcement. My father's voice boomed through the house as he shouted his question to my mum. "Ay? Ay? Is it ready?"

I didn't like the way she was being treated but kept my thoughts under my breath. I was hungry, to be fair, and knew enough about diplomacy to not jeopardise a good plateful of whatever Mum had cooked up.

I kept my comment short. "Ay? That is what camels eat."

Mum heard, grinned and put her finger to her lips. She motioned to me and Grandad to take a seat. Dad entered the room without taking in what was going on. He hadn't adjusted his volume. "When's dinner ready, Ay? I'm starving."

"Now, Manny. Right now. Sit down. I'm pleased you're hungry." Her management of him was expertly achieved.

I caught her eye as I added my comment. "Me too, Mum. The harvest is huge this year. So much work."

Grandad patted his tummy and grinned. "Take my advice, boys. Store it well, like I do. You're going to need it."

Mum was about to summon Shaz when she strolled in. "I'm hungry too, Mum. Someone rattled Jezebel's cage today. The girls felt the force of her foul mood."

Grandad put his arm round her. "I heard that from Joel."

Dad was scathing with his father. "Wasting time with the likes of him won't get you far, Dad. What does he know?"

Grandad wasn't giving him the last word. "Quite a lot, actually. He says there's going to be a great famine."

It wasn't the last word. Dad's retort stung. "Was he singing about that to music? He's a compulsive lyre plucker, remember."

Shaz went on the defensive. "Dad, he's very talented. Don't skit at him like that."

Dad stared at us, one at a time and measured his words. "I'll take him seriously when he does a proper day's work."

Grandad sensed victory. "Well, if Joel is right about the famine, never you mind about a proper day's labour. You won't have much to work with. Neither will Eran."

I attempted to lighten the tone. "Sounds good to me."

Grandad remained serious. "Look, Joel's boss has been to see the king. He gave his Majesty the message and it seems he had to exit stage left pretty hastily thereafter. The queen got in on the scene too."

Dad scratched his head and made an interesting observation. "She's into Baal as her religion, isn't she? Baal specialises in weather, if I remember correctly."

Grandad "Son, why is Elijah on the run if that's the case? Wouldn't the queen just think Baal had the solution to a famine?"

Shaz shook her head. "The queen doesn't like any whiff of

opposition, Grandad. That's why she was so horrible today. The girl doing her make-up felt the rough edge of her tongue."

I laughed. "Is there a cream for that too, Shaz? The queen really doesn't do things by halves!"

She pulled a face. "Haha! You know what I mean. Listen, that musician who disappeared hasn't come back. There's a rumour he's been killed. The girls say that she's so dangerous right now."

Dad set his expression to that of one bearing wisdom. "Don't jump to conclusions so hastily, and don't you be saying that in other company, Sharon. You'll be next to disappear if you are not careful. If she prays to Baal, I'm sure she'll get any food supply chain issues resolved. That's what Baal does."

Mum's voice was slightly raised. "I'm not alone in suspecting Baal requires more than someone asking him nicely. There are rumours of the odd child sacrifice as well as all sorts of other unpalatable demands. Soup, anyone?"

I couldn't miss this one. "Baal's in her court, right?"

Dad nearly cracked a smile and for a few moments, he was the father I remembered before he changed. "Witty, Sunshine, very witty. That god's divine answer might drive her round the bend."

"That'd be a curve Baal, Dad." I'd got him on less controversial territory as the atmosphere lightened.

He bit his lip to disguise a grin. "You're on form, Son. What's it called when that god is small and floating in a crib among the river reeds?"

"Basket Baal?"

Mum laughed out loud. "Boys, what about when he looks completely at his best?"

I went for the clean sweep. "Nice one Mother! Super Baal."

Grandad brought verbal sobriety back to the table. "Not wishing to be a wet blanket, but there's a man gone missing, maybe murdered. This kind of direct royal intervention is no laughing matter."

His son was dismissive. "It's all talk, Dad. Take no notice. Anyway, royalty does what has to be done, brutal or not."

Grandad's tone was precise. "Manny, the Lord does the talking. Baal doesn't exist. He's a figment of your imagination. And stop leading your family astray too!"

I've had to do a lot of growing up quite quickly of late, although I harboured a hankering for the times with Dad when he wasn't like this. I wanted to be in a normal family. That didn't seem to be happening, so the rebel in me kicked in. I convinced myself that I was old enough to make decisions for myself about deities.

"Hang on there, Grandad, I'll make my own mind up."

Mum's facial expression turned to mild disapproval. "Whatever. Superstitious nonsense, most of it."

I felt a pang of guilt, compelling me to explain myself. "I must say that I like the idea of a loving God. I think there might be one, probably the Lord. But I'm struggling why He would send a famine to His chosen people. I don't get that."

Shaz had an idea. "Joel must get it, or he wouldn't write songs to Him. Why don't you ask him? I'd come with you. I'm puzzled too."

I couldn't stop myself. "If Joel's boss can hear directly from the Lord, I'll wait for the Lord to contact me. Or at least show me a sign. A big one."

Shaz smirked. She knew I'd gone too far. "That's not your

true attitude, Eran, is it? Open eyes, open ears, open mind, eh?"

Grandad held up a hand. "Your comments are the best thing I've heard tonight, Sharon. Well put!"

Mum brought us all back to earth. "Soup, anyone? It's going cold."

9

ZAREPHATH

It was about six weeks later in the city square when Grandad next saw Joel. Much water had flowed in that time under the bridge over Jezreel's River Kishon. When he returned home that evening, Grandad was full of important news to impart. He and I sat down to catch up.

"Eran, guess who I bumped into today?"

"Let me think. Probably not the queen. Give me a clue."

"Lyre."

I paused and acknowledged his grin. "Ah. And how is my friend Joel? I haven't clapped eyes on the chap for a while."

"It's not good, Eran. His mood and demeanour were pretty grim."

"That's not against the law, Grandad. He can't be good-looking and cheerful all the time."

"Your sister wouldn't agree with that one, Eran. But seriously, Joel is having to move around cautiously at present. I think he's scared."

"Joel? Scared? How could someone as nice as him have enemies?"

Grandad coped with my inappropriate flippancy. "It's real. Elijah is still missing. It's a month and a half now."

"Okay, but how does that affect Joel?"

"Jezebel will have a strategy to make the most of his absence. Any purge could start with Elijah's students. And that includes Joel."

"I should have realised that, Grandad. Sorry. Have they no idea where Elijah has gone? Is he still alive?"

"Apparently, a traveller had come by yesterday. He reported seeing a man who matched Elijah's description around a place called the Kerith Ravine."

"That's to the east of Jordan, isn't it?"

"That's the one. The man he saw emerged from a cave when he came out for sustenance, so he had a word with him. He told the traveller something odd."

"What?" I was blunt.

"He claimed a few birds dropped food off to him at the cavern entrance. He showed him a small flock of them close by, beside a brook. His feathered friends had stopped for a swift drink and a quick bath."

I couldn't help myself. "Wow! Home delivery! There's an idea for the future!"

Grandad shrugged. "Well, I asked Joel if we needed to get someone out to him. He told me not to hold my breath. Apparently, the brook was dried up after they'd had a few sips and a speedy splash. But it's possible that Elijah's on the move again by now."

I was alarmed. "Back here? It's unsafe! She'll have his guts for corset fasteners."

"No, Joel's story was that he was moving towards the

coast. He's headed for the seaside. He told the traveller that the Lord had commanded him to hot foot it over there. There was a place prepared for him in the home of a widow and her son."

"All to escape the grip of our dear queen. Right?"

"I guess so, Eran. The town is called Zarephath." Grandad yawned. "I don't like the feel of what's happening right now. Purge or no purge, the palace appears to have been overwhelmed by unconstrained evil, and it won't end well for anyone. Keep your head down, my boy, and pray to the Lord that He will restore justice and peace to this city."

When Grandad told me to pray to the Lord, I did just that. Six weeks of seven-day working in the fields meant I had little contact with anyone but the family, but on the morning of my forty-third successive early morning start, I had a question for my father. "Dad, can I take a week off? I'm laboured out."

He stared at me. "No way, Son. We own some of the country's most fertile fields and we've lost three of our farmhands in the last two weeks. There's too much to do. Sorry, but it's an impossibility."

This was the first I'd heard of it. "Can't we just get them back? Is it a matter of more pay?"

"I wish it was, Eran. There's no sign of them anywhere. I've been asking around. Three fit lads."

Grandad was listening with interest, so I tried another line of enquiry. "Grandad, have they been to the city square? You'd spot them, they're just a few years older than me."

He wasn't much help. "I've been there sparingly myself. When I did go, there were fewer and fewer of the older regulars gathering there, never mind any youngsters. I've not heard of anyone looking for work, if that's what you mean. It has been hot for ages now, with no relief through rain, but that doesn't explain matters either."

There was a dark cloud, however, but this one was hovering metaphorically over our conversation. I looked around. "Where's Shaz? She's always home by now."

Dad shook his head and grinned. "Must be working late. She'll be blaming the queen, as usual."

Grandad saw the look on my face. "Manny, she's over an hour late. I'm going to walk up towards the palace. She may be approaching adulthood, but to me, she's still her grandad's little girl. See you in a few minutes."

Dad waited until he had gone. "Close the door, Eran. Check he's gone."

I did. "He's gone alright. Why the secrecy?"

"Son, I'll be honest. I'm starting to worry about the rain. I don't want any more of his nonsense about the Lord. The Lord's his answer to everything. Look, will you pray to Baal with me? Your family is at risk, and your mum's not having any of it. Do your duty, eh?"

I couldn't. "But I don't believe in Baal. I don't believe in anyone yet, not for sure."

Dad pulled a face. "You're just like so many youngsters, nailing your colours firmly to the fence. Baal does weather. Just try praying to him. It might work. It could save us."

Mum would not have been so confident. I was ruffled. "How can I pray to a god in whom I don't believe, Dad?"

Dad was nothing if not pragmatic. "I can't see a problem there, Son. You just speak it out and see if anyone gets back to you. You and me both."

To be honest, I was a bit spooked by the weather. We farmers rely on it. I heard myself agreeing. "Okay, when Grandad's not around. Tomorrow in the fields."

I glanced outside and spotted two figures I knew so well. "Say nothing, he's coming back. He's got Shaz. He's helping her walk! She's all white, like she's seen a ghost!"

10

TRENCH

Dad smirked. "Women, hey? What are they like! What's she got to whinge about this time? Come on, let's bring the pair of them in and hear whatever drivel young Sharon has to share."

I was thrown by his uncaring stance on his own daughter's distress. I resolved to do what he should have done. I took her arm and sat her down. "What's up, Shaz?"

She couldn't speak. I took my other option. "What's the matter with her, Grandad?" I glanced at his face. "And you look dreadful too!"

Grandad drew a deep breath. "You aren't going to like this, Eran. Your dad won't either. I'm feeling sick in the pit of my stomach."

Mum walked in. I did something I hadn't done since I was a kid. I held her hand. Together, we took Shaz to her room, where Mum motioned to me to leave the two of them. Reluctantly, I shuffled back, wondering what I was going to hear.

Dad had been waiting for my return, which only served to intensify my anxiety. He normally blundered on regardless. He bit his lip before addressing his own father. "Come on Dad, tell it as it is. We can take it."

We? He might have, but I didn't know if I could.

Grandad related what Shaz had told him in the little time they had had. "So the queen had been absent for a while with some male visitors. They'd annoyed her, it seems. Anyway, she sent for a girl to bring some make-up, and Shaz was given it. She set off with it, only to find that the king was at the palace door. Shaz went out round the back, heard a struggle and hid. Then it stopped and she saw some soldiers digging in the field behind."

Dad assumed that attitude of self-righteousness we all loved so dearly. Not. "I knew this would be something and nothing. Digging is allowed, isn't it?"

Mum walked in as Grandad took his time. He acknowledged her with a slight bow.

She spoke first. "I heard your conversation from Sharon's room. The military were excavating to make graves, I'm guessing."

Grandad nodded vigorously. "Manny, Ayala is right. Trench-digging is fine for soldiers, but when there are dead bodies to bury in it by the palace, that's not something or nothing. Poor Sharon saw it all from where she was hiding."

Dad's next words were toxic. "Enemies of the state need to be eradicated, whoever they are. That's what soldiers are for. You know that better than anyone."

Grandad summoned up all his reserves of patience. "I did my time in the army and saw a lot of sights I never wish to see again, but this is different. Sharon recognised those bodies. She'd seen the three men on your land, Manny."

At that moment, Sharon returned, pale-faced and drawn, to hear my father's answer. "Trespassers, robbers, good-for-nothing thieves, I bet. I say good on the authorities for teaching them a lesson. Scum of the earth, these types."

Grandad's voice rose as he lost it. "Manny, they were your men. Your hired hands. The word around the junior palace staff is that they were murdered because Jezebel invited them to what we might delicately call a sensual group activity, and it wasn't a game of charades. The three of them refused. Jezebel's public shaming was not something she could countenance, even if she'd come on to them one at a time. But the queen suggesting a foursome? She called for the guards, lied to them that they'd tried to rape her, and ordered their murder."

Dad's pride wouldn't let him react as a decent human being, but he gulped. I couldn't believe it was his own workers who had been taken out, and yet he showed no compassion. "They were foolish, and they paid the price. They obviously misread the queen's intentions. I'll get replacements for the farm, don't you worry!"

Did he wink at Sharon before he stormed out? Pouring scorn on her trauma was one thing, but he had no need to compound it in this way. Why can't he be like he used to be?

Her colour returned somewhat, but her words were still few. I hadn't seen such distress before, and I never want to see it again. Mum had heard everything, and when I went to her, her tears flowed with ours. What kind of a monster was our dad?

11

SCAREMONGERING

Family relationships with my father proved almost impossible to rebuild over the next few days. Meals were taken in silence whenever he was there, broken only by his stilted attempts at conversation to which no-one would respond. It was horrible. Sharon's trauma, our trauma, was not for discussion, and not a word was mentioned about those poor men.

Eventually, he melted. Partially, at least. "I'm sorry if you don't like my opinions. I don't hold them to hurt you, I promise. It's just that when you aren't dealing with truth, it is my responsibility as the head of the family to put you right. I would be deserting my duty if I did otherwise."

Grandad took the potential olive branch, but there was a gentle chiding in it. "Perhaps it's how you do it, Manny."

Mum was suffering. "Are you sure what the truth is, Manny? It's like you've been brainwashed. Promise me you'll think it over?"

He spoke softly for once. "No need, Ay. I'm right."

It was kicking off again, albeit politely. Grandad found a

smile from somewhere, but it failed to achieve his anticipated diplomatic de-escalation.

"Listen, Manny, people are speaking about more and more folks going missing from town. Older, younger, men, women. All walks of life. I'm telling you, they're saying that there's a campaign to stamp out anyone with a belief in Yahweh. And a whisper from a neighbour is all it takes."

Dad sat back and spread out his palms. "Believe me, all of you, we're in the grip of a crime wave, that's all. They get what they deserve. We've just got to get through it."

Grandad kept his cool. "Do you know why poor Sharon was so scared when she came back with me a few days ago? She's still frightened now. If anyone saw Sharon hiding that day, one whisper from someone who has taken against her and she's facing the unthinkable. Then our family will be targeted, including you."

I don't like scaremongering, but this was different. Insecurity is a blight on life. Was I wrong, or was my dad aligning himself with the perpetrators of hatred? What was going on? Would it backfire on him, and us? I didn't know.

Later, I told Grandad my thoughts. He put his arm around me and smiled. "Stay calm, Eran. And pray."

I don't suppose he slept all that well that night. With the exception of Dad, none of us did either. Dad was still blustering on in the morning. I could see Grandad's face and was not surprised when he grabbed a coat and headed out. It was early afternoon when he returned. I asked him where he had been.

"I've been sitting in the city square, Eran. Just passing the time of day. I was on my own to start with. None of my old friends come out anymore, but young Joel spotted me."

"Joel? What did he have to say?"

"He was sporting a big new scarf, which was odd, but he pointed at my coat and asked why I'd brought it. I told him that at my age, you can get cold in a heatwave. He had thought it was some kind of disguise."

"Disguise? Your coat?"

"That puzzled me until he explained the scarf. It was to hide his face. He'd received a visit from Obadiah, advising him to keep out of the public spotlight and give the music a rest. Mind you, Joel informed me that he'd stopped a while back."

"At least that's one less thing for Dad to complain about, Grandad."

Grandad opened his palms. "If only he'd been listening to the words. Shall I tell you more of what Joel told me?"

I nodded. "He lowered his voice, Eran, and muttered that we live in dark times. Obadiah says he may need to go into hiding one day, out of the way. Caution must be the watchword. He's walking a tricky path at the palace these days."

"Did Joel report any news of Elijah?"

"Very much so. There are rumours on the grapevine of remarkable events in Zarephath, according to Obadiah. The Lord is moving, Eran."

"How do you know it's God, Grandad? I wish I had your faith."

"You will, Eran. Hear this! Elijah has been given more food."

"He's a hungry man, Grandad. If he's in Zarephath, they'll have supplies there."

"Think, Eran. You recall Elijah was heading for a widow's home? You know what a widow is?"

I screwed up my face. It was more like my father's type of stupid question, but I answered because it was from Grandad. "It's a woman whose husband has passed away."

"True, but I meant more than that, Eran. The answer is poor. Widows are usually living in great poverty. So having an extra mouth to feed is a huge burden."

"Okay, I get it. So did Joel's boss get fed or not?"

"He did, Eran. He went to the house, then took her last loaf of bread in the world and scoffed it. Right in front of her young son."

I couldn't stop myself. "Doesn't say much for the Lord, if I'm honest. How bad did that woman feel? Elijah? In God's name, how could he do such a thing?"

"Steady on, Eran. Remember the brook and the birds? Elijah knew something even more special was about to happen. The lady's cupboards were miraculously filled with all the flour and oil that they needed, and it keeps happening."

"Dad wouldn't like that happening here, Grandad."

"Why not, Eran? He might lose interest in Baal if he saw that."

Grandad saw the beginnings of a smile twitch across my features. "If the Lord does that on a wider scale, he'll put Dad out of business!"

He grinned. "Take a step back if you can, Eran. You will see how we know that the Lord is on the move."

12

CANNIBAL

Two years went by. We survived. Dad still went to his business meetings, but the workload reduced along with our food stocks.

As expected, Joel disappeared from view. He wasn't at home. He wasn't at work, obviously, but no-one was overly concerned. Many of our city residents had closed their social shutters. It was generally assumed that Joel and his peers had been taken into the military. Sharon, however, who was still attending her workplace, heard a rumour among the junior staff there that an official there had secretly arranged for a group of around a hundred faithfuls to go into hiding, and was getting them fed and watered from palace supplies.

The theory brought scorn from senior sources, who stated that they'd joined the army like the rest of them. Any such subterfuge would inevitably have been noticed by Obadiah, although that would have left him in a very tricky position.

On the domestic front, Mum was hardly eating. She'd never been overweight, but now, at times, to me she looked emaciated. Grandad came into the room. He read my mind.

"Famine is terrible, Eran." Grandad sat me down. "It starts by hurting the poor. They can't buy what they need. Crime rates rise along with hunger. Then prices rise further as scarcity tightens its noose. Animals have to be killed, and eventually, the ones we don't usually eat. Then it's insects, anything to assuage hunger. The rich are the only people not to be affected until severity reaches extremes. Then we get to hear stories of cannibalism, and people eating their own children, just to survive."

"Grandad, how can the Lord permit that?" I remained stuck on the issue. Nothing about it fitted my image of how He should do things.

"Eran, you have to understand that the Lord hates sin. He detests it utterly, and He has to punish it. Justice demands that the penalty be measured according to the seriousness of our rebellion as a people. He chose our nation for Himself and look how we are paying Him back."

I took a deep breath. "I need some time with that one, Grandad. It's hard to understand."

Famine continued to dominate domestic life. I was in the hallway when I overheard my parents talking in the kitchen the next day and was perplexed by Dad's attitude. Mum had just explained her worries to him, and he was quite dismissive.

"I'm doing my best, Ay. Don't go on about it. I know we've used most of what we saved. There's nothing I can do about it. There's never been a time like it. The land is as dry as a bone. Nothing's growing."

Mum was on the verge of tears. "Manny, they've got food at the palace. You've got connections. You're in there often enough."

Dad shook his head. "Can't Sharon ask? She's a bit of a favourite with the queen, I gather, from what they say. She could possibly pull a few of Jezebel's strings."

Grandad had overheard too. He pushed past me, knocked and went in to where they were talking. "Manny, Sharon lives in fear of the woman. I'm telling you; she's not going to ask. Over my dead body. And you know what, I'm not sure I could eat anything the queen deigned to send us."

I went in too, followed closely by my sister who had sensed a conflict from her room. Grandad realised she must have heard his words. He smiled. "Right, Sharon?"

Shaz shrugged. "Jezebel? She…"

She was about to say more but got no further as Dad supervened. "Queen Jezebel, please. What's wrong with your generation? Show some respect."

I was bristling but Shaz kept her composure. "The food's alright, Grandad. That's why I've taken more hours despite the mental strains. It's so I can get fed there, sometimes twice a day. Then I don't need food at home if I skip breakfast."

I had an idea. "Shaz, do they throw food away? The royal table is always groaning under the weight of what's on it, if I'm right."

Dad hadn't finished. "Rightly so. What's your point, Eran?"

I told him. "Isn't the best thing to ask the palace cooks, Dad? Shaz will know them for sure and might feel up to approaching them. Eh, Shaz?"

"I'll keep my eye open for any opportunities, but there'll be other girls with similar ideas. And don't forget, even the chefs have families. Jezebel has a grip of iron on everything and everyone. I'll do what I can."

Mum raised a finger. "No risks, Shaz, please. We should listen to the faithfuls. They say we'll all get through this if we trust the Lord."

Dad was fuming. "Ay, whose side are you on? Eran's already complaining of hunger when we're in the fields. There's only us two these days. There's not that much to do until Baal sends the rain. Eran and I pray to him."

Grandad couldn't accept that. "You're a bigger fool than I thought, Manny."

Did I pray to Baal? Really? I always stood silent when Dad invoked Baal, but from my side, I have a sense of helplessness. To me, both Baal and the Lord seem to be on sabbatical right now.

My thoughts were cut short by my grandfather. "Baal isn't there, Manny. There's no such person. The Lord has sent a sign to His people. He's fed Elijah. He's sustained him. We need to ask ourselves why."

Dad banged the table. "Not the Lord again, please. There'd be no famine if he was real."

Shaz tried the conciliatory approach which had failed before. "Isn't the Lord worth a try, Dad, for all of our sakes?"

He stared her full in the face, his eyes burning. "Just don't hold your breath."

I thought I spotted her screwing up her nose at his reply, but she turned to Grandad. Clever girl, I thought, she's right, don't bait Dad. She was smarter than I had appreciated. She smilingly ignored him.

"What you said before has given me an idea, Grandad. I just might be able to help."

Mum was in straightaway. "Shaz, no risks."

"No risks, Mum."

"You mean about asking the cooks, Sharon?" Grandad raised his eyebrows in anticipation of an affirmative.

He got one. "If the cooks sent it on their own initiative, it wouldn't be from the queen, Grandad. It's a question of my picking the right moment."

Dad's face was a picture of confusion. He was unsure if she'd outflanked him or proved him right. Grandad winked at my sister. "If your plan works, Sharon, I'll ask the Lord not to drop off the food via raven post. A bag or two left by a human on the doorstep would be fine."

For the next few days, no delivery occurred by ornithological or terrestrial means. No-one spoke about it much, but Dad's self-righteous expectant expression irritated Mum as much as the rest of us.

One evening, Dad could hold out no longer. "Any luck with your plan, Shaz?"

She shrugged. "Maybe. The queen required a facial yesterday and I got to do it. I was in on my own with her. She relaxed like I've never seen her before."

Mum exhaled sharply. "Weren't you afraid?"

"At first, Mum, and I was so nervous throughout, but then two strange events happened."

Dad was keen to move on. "Never mind all that, did you wind up getting a food order in?"

Sharon shook her head. He emitted a heavy sigh.

I smiled encouragingly. "You were waiting to speak to the kitchen staff, not Queen J., as I recall, Shaz."

She nodded. "Yes. And before you ask, Dad, I can't simply pop in to see the men in the kitchen during my downtime in the palace. Everything there is so tightly controlled. Food, conversations, staff movements, the lot."

Grandad had been listening closely. "Sharon, love, tell us about what occurred when the queen was so relaxed. She must have had faith in your skills to be like that. What took place?"

"Firstly, she started chatting to me, woman to woman. She asked where I lived."

Mum looked pleased. "Lovely. I hope you told her it was a nice home."

Sharon cracked a brief smile. "I did. And I told her about Grandad too. I told her he was very special to me and that I love him to bits."

Dad appeared rather miffed. "I hope you mentioned me. I'm one of her biggest fans."

"A bit. I told her you prayed to Baal to send rain, with Eran. She almost purred when she heard that."

Dad drew himself up to his full height. Pride was written right across his features.

"You told her we'd prayed to Baal? She'd have liked that. Did she ask you anything else?"

"Only who else lived here. She wanted to know about Mum."

"The queen? Asked about me? Wow!"

"She asked if you were a faithful."

Mum's face changed. "How did you answer that?"

"By telling her how lovely you are, Mum. I said I thought you were a quiet, trusting follower of the Lord. I shook all over when she frowned at me after she heard those words. I quickly added that you tolerated other gods like Baal and Asherah and wondered how powerful they might be."

"How did you respond to the frown?"

"I managed to smile. Then she smiled back. She told me that my mum sounded lovely."

It was Dad's self-esteem which was bursting. "Well played, Shaz. My daughter is friends with the queen. So, when will we get some food out of this?"

"She asked how we were coping with the famine, if we had food at home, Dad."

"What did you tell her?"

"I let her know that we could do with some."

Dad looked perplexed. "And she refused? You are telling us you hadn't got anywhere with a food request, yet you had her eating out of the palm of your hand. And you'd mentioned Baal and Asherah. What went wrong? Was she displeased with you for asking?"

Shaz paused a moment and stared him full in the face. "She said to tell Mum that Baal would see to it."

Dad banged his fist on the table and stormed out. Grandad, though, had another question.

"What about the second event, Sharon? What was that about?"

"Oh yes. Just before we finished, there was a knock on the door. It was a young man, bringing her a plate of food. There were all kinds of gourmet snacks on it. He put it on the table and left without a word, or even looking at either of us."

Grandad scratched his head. "Why did that surprise you, Sharon?"

She pulled a pained expression before speaking. "It was Joel."

Was the face because Joel didn't acknowledge her? Was it

fear of speaking out of turn? Was it Jezebel's aura? I didn't know where to begin.

Mum spotted it. "Joel's not been around for quite a while. Let's be glad he's okay."

Shaz sniffed. There was more to all this than met my eye, I was sure. I didn't sleep too well that night. Jezebel was never short of domestic servants to do her bidding, so why another one? Why him? But Mum was usually right. And maybe, just maybe, Shaz could speak to Joel and get some food for us all. If she couldn't, I could. Or so I thought.

13

MUCKY

It appeared that Shaz had made quite an impression on Jezza, as my sister and I had started to call her new best mate. The queen has only gone and sent for Shaz again some ten days later, another facial, and they'd talked some more. The rations were thinner than ever at home, and I hadn't clapped eyes on Joel in town. Would I have to hang around near the palace? Security precluded.

Dad had to know more about this latest royal encounter. "Spill the beans, Shaz."

Me? I'd have killed for a few beans at that moment. So would Grandad, who'd just joined the rest of us.

Shaz acquiesced. "I asked what she thought about the weather."

Dad winced. "Not wise."

"I didn't mean anything by it, just making conversation. She doesn't make me so anxious anymore when I'm with her. I just chat as I make her look amazingly beautiful. It's simple."

"Sharon, that is not how you speak to the queen. Look, how did she respond?"

Grandad frowned until he heard her response, which restored a twinkle to his eye. She waved a hand dismissively in his direction. "Don't worry. You don't know what you're talking about, Dad. It's girls' talk. She laughed and asked me for my opinion."

"And what wisdom did you dispense on matters meteorological, might I ask?" Dad was getting wound up, and her next words added fuel to the fire.

"I made it clear that I didn't know a lot, but it was obvious we had to break this weather, Dad. I said that for me, Baal's not cutting the mustard with his speed of response. She was so charming to me that I thought, you know what, here's the chance. So, I took it."

He was edging towards fury. "You didn't push your old grandad's Lord God as an option? Tell me no!"

"I did. I thought it might help. I added that older people were often wiser, and that Grandad cared so much about me as well as others."

The hackles were right up. I felt ashamed to hear my father bark at her. "Was she angry?"

I sensed her tears weren't far away, but she held it together. "Not really. She smiled again, agreed that Baal didn't seem to be in a rush, then added that she'd give it some thought." She looked around the room. "Why, have I done something wrong?"

It became obvious that no answer was forthcoming. He slammed the door behind him before she had finished.

Grandad sighed. "Sharon, you were very brave, my dear. Very brave. Was that it? Did she say anything else?"

His reply relieved me of the burden I thought would be mine.

"Yes. She told me that if you went up to the palace next Friday, she'd give you a hamper, Grandad, for being so kind to me. I knew I could do it."

Mum managed a grin. "Nice one Shaz. If only your father knew."

I returned to my room. My relief was short-lived. Joel was the future of provender provision at this house, not Jezza. We needed regular deliveries, not a one-off gift. Then I felt ungrateful. People were dying of hunger, and I was picking my provider. But more importantly, I had to get to Joel.

The next day, he appeared. Not where I was, but in the city square. It had been relatively empty, of course, since the crackdowns began, but Grandad figured out that his age brought immunity and strolled up that way to see what was occurring. It seems that, coming the other way, was Joel. That evening, Grandad and I took a short walk and when no-one was in earshot, he told me of his encounter.

Joel had been greeted warmly, as Grandad always does. Our musician friend replied in a friendly way, after a hesitant, wary start. He didn't call him Grandad, like before, though.

"Why was that, Grandad?" I needed to know.

"Don't know, Eran. It was a long time ago now, back when you and your sister were around that he called me Grandad. Everyone's cautious of their relationships these days. Walls have ears and all that. And maybe there was no one to impress."

"You mean Shaz?"

"It seems to me he may have lost interest there, if he ever had one."

"Oh, he did, Grandad. Maybe he's been avoiding her. He

couldn't speak to Shaz when Jezebel was with her. Maybe he has just fallen out with Shaz."

"It happens, Eran."

"Yes. Did Joel talk about food, Grandad?"

"Only the same way as everyone does. He was reticent. He looked quite well fed, if I'm honest. I did ask him about his work."

"Ah! Did he mention the palace? Did he deny he'd seen Shaz?"

"He told me he'd not been there long. Domestic service, you know, below stairs, usually out of sight."

"No hint, then, about his encounter with Shaz?"

"To be honest, I didn't bring that up."

"Why not, Grandad?"

"It wasn't the moment. I couldn't risk embarrassing him. Anyway, he hurried away."

The fact that I had to be the one to approach Joel on the pressing matter of supplies slapped me in the face. I had a feeling that there were bridges to mend elsewhere, ones which I hadn't burnt.

I sighed. Grandad was the man I trusted above all others. "Grandad, will this dismal period ever end? We've all taken a battering, haven't we?"

He smiled. "We're still here, Eran. Let's be thankful for the Lord's protection."

I wasn't, really. I thought it was all coincidence. He saw my eyes and read my mind. "Listen, Jezebel will never stop the word of the Lord. Politics is a mucky business for sure, and they don't come much muckier than our dear queen and her hubby, but what we are going through is temporary."

I could see that, but it didn't help. I had a further question. "What about Obadiah? Is he managing to hold the line? Did Joel mention him?"

"No, Eran. I've heard that they've tried to put the frighteners on him. Not that it will work in his case, but he's watched everywhere he goes. Jezebel and her evil lacky of a husband have murdered community leaders who promote the Lord, but there seems to be an invisible force which protects Obadiah. You can see that in his character and his demeanour. He seems to be untouchable."

"How do you know that's true? Joel won't be able to verify that anyway, if either of us sees him again. He won't see much of what's going on from below stairs."

"One of the security guards is a chap who used to spend the time with regulars in the square. His son might have been a friend of yours when you were little. The word is that he's a faithful, with no time for the Baal nonsense. Either way, someone's been leaking the truth from the palace to the local grapevine, and it reaches my ears."

"I wish I had your faith in the Lord, Grandad. You are so sure of your words."

"You will do, Eran. Would it help if I told you about Elijah? The news is from the same source."

"Elijah? Is he coming back to Jezreel?"

Grandad wagged a finger in my direction. "Not exactly. He's the topic of much gossip at the seaside, though. And I don't mean with the widow. Before you say anything, she's a bit old for him."

I laughed, but his next statement floored me.

"Eran, it's her son. He died."

My reaction was instinctive. "So, Elijah's staying there to look after her?"

"No, he did rather better than that. With the Lord's help, he brought the boy back to life. That's why I am sure of what I say. Our God is active. He is good."

"Hang on Grandad, was he properly dead? Or in a coma?"

"Eran, Elijah knows dead when he sees it. He stretched over him and prayed to the Lord."

"And?" I was still struggling to see this was real.

"The Lord did the business. Now the woman holds her tenant in awe and knows the one and only God. Can you see the Lord's hand in this? Here's Jezebel kicking off big time against all things to do with Him. In Jezreel we are cowering in fear. So, our God shows His mighty power for good, to save the lad. He's started with the poorest. Jezebel's evil regime kills whilst the Lord offers life."

"Does Joel know any of this? And does he know about your palace mole? Did he hint at anything at all?"

"No, nothing. I hope he doesn't, for his own sake."

"Grandad, it's so tough making guesses when all we need is truth."

"I agree, Eran, it's desperate, to be honest. Every situation is a potential trap. But we do have a hamper to look forward to."

"We do, this Friday. Thanks to Shaz! I'm going to make sure Mum gets her share of food as well."

"Good lad. I'll let you know when I've collected it. Mind you, it does feel like crumbs from under a rich woman's table, eh? We're like the palace dogs." He grinned. "Rations for us dogs of war, Eran, in a spiritual battle."

I nodded enthusiastically but deep down, I wasn't sure. I felt the discomfort, yet did I really understand about a spiritual battle? No. I just loved the man. Then something awful hit me. He saw the colour leave my cheeks.

"What's up, Eran?"

"Grandad, what if it's a trick? The hamper business, I mean."

He laughed. "Ah, you mean the queen will have poisoned the contents. That's in the realms of a fairy tale, not the real world, Eran. Anyway, you can taste everything first for us!"

"I'm serious, Grandad. Our family needs you. You're the rock on which it is built."

He took my hand. "Look here, young man, what concern is an old fellow like me to Queen Jezebel? She must have a soft under-belly somewhere. But thank you for your concern."

I didn't like the way we'd ended. My urge to speak to Joel became even more pressing. My family needed him. Whether I liked it or not, the only way to reach him was via Sharon.

14

COPIOUS

It was late in the evening when I tapped on her door. She motioned me in. Dad was snoring for Israel in the matrimonial chamber, as he used to call it in the days when he had a sense of humour, but still we kept our voices to a whisper over what must have been half an hour. Then, to finalise our plan and keep Grandad out of danger, I needed to know when her next session with Jezza was set for.

It was in fact the next morning, after the usual copious royal breakfast. Shaz was to choose the right moment to thank the queen again for the promised hamper, then ask if I could speak to someone from the kitchen to see if Grandad could really manage to carry her wonderful gift, at his advanced age. Even Jezebel couldn't refuse that, could she?

First, though, how would I be there? I wouldn't, to be exact. I'd be outside. Before then, at first light, I was to stroll as casually as I could manage in front of the building until a guard challenged me. Remember, this guy would have been on duty all night. I would smile and say I was the brother of Jezza's top beautician, and I had a romantic message for Joel.

Sharon was happy with that. It should work a treat. The guard would ensure that once the royal command had been received in the kitchen, it would be Joel who carried out the queen's bidding and bring the hamper to where I would be waiting.

It was a masterplan. Security would know Joel was following a royal command and would let him be. I wouldn't be causing an issue for security, as I was outside the palace grounds. Grandad was right. Jezebel did have a soft underbelly, and I knew I'd found it.

I rehearsed my lines as Joel's time would be limited. I needed to know why he had abandoned my sister, why he had been cooler with Grandad, and whether he could get us a source of food. Oh, and my secret role which was to tell him that Sharon loved him. No pressure there, then.

I returned to my room to catch up with a bit of sleep, then I heard Shaz getting ready to leave for work.

Half an hour later, without a word to anyone else, I headed for the palace square and took up my position.

Joel arrived, but he was not alone. That was not our plan. The queen had beaten us to it. I improvised. I greeted him warmly and nodded to the guard whose helmet was covering much of his face whilst allowing him to be watching fastidiously and hearing all the conversations around him. His expression, such as I could discern, remained fixed. He was unflinching. Joel's eyes were telling me to get on with it.

"What's this hamper business, Eran? What's so special about your family?"

I looked him in the eye. "The queen ordered it. Grandad is convinced it is the Lord sending it, not the queen."

He made to move away. "Are you wasting my time?"

This was not the friend I'd defended when my father was on his case. "Joel, why are you being like this? Are you struggling with something?"

He remained resolute. "I've come down to discuss a hamper, not wallow in self-pity."

It wasn't going how I'd imagined. I tried another tack. "We loved your music, Joel. Except for my dad. We've missed you."

Joel shook his head. "I follow Baal, like my queen. Tell that grandad of yours that he's deluded."

"He's not. He is always talking about the Lord, even in this awful crackdown. He loves the Lord, Joel, like you used to."

"And the rest of you?"

"Dad's still trying Baal out, Mum keeps quiet, and Sharon's still in love with you."

This time he did move away. "Wait there. I'll bring you a loaf of bread."

I regret what I did next, but I shouted after him. "Forget it, Joel, if that's all the help you can manage."

It was so stupid. He didn't even look back. He couldn't, as I figured afterwards. He disappeared back into the palace, gesturing and shaking his head. I'd blown it. What an idiot I had been. It felt like the end of all hope.

My great plan had flopped disastrously. I couldn't find the strength to face the family. I sought refuge in my room, feeling that I was at the bottom of a deep pit, with no way out. My friendship with Joel was over. Sharon would be horrified at how I had handled it all. Dad would be furious at me for losing the promised hamper, and Mum? She'd say nothing but would still be sacrificially hungry. And Grandad? He would be hurting because I'd failed to seek his wisdom. There was nothing left which I could do in my own strength. I lay still, endlessly replaying the incident in my head. The potential fallout was total.

It wasn't till late afternoon that I ventured down. Mum looked at me strangely. That could have been all I needed to send me right back where I'd come from, but before I could turn on my heels, she had a question.

"Eran, I thought you were out with Grandad. Have you been here all day?"

"I didn't feel too well, Mum. Is Grandad in?"

"I heard the door go before we got up this morning, heard voices and assumed you and he had gone to the fields for some reason. I haven't seen him all day. Can you go and check his room?"

I did. It was empty. The bed was unmade, which was odd. He was usually very tidy.

A few minutes later, Shaz came in from work. I heard Mum ask if she'd seen him around the city on her way back, as he sometimes went to meet her. The reply was in the negative.

15

BESOTTED

Dad returned a while after that conversation. He was not in the best frame of mind, but as usual, we didn't know why. Shaz smiled at him and asked him the pressing question.

"Any sign of Grandad, Dad?"

Dad was short. "Sharon, you know your grandad hasn't worked on the land since he did his back in years ago. And how would I have seen him anyway if I'd been out on the farm all day?"

There was something about the 'if' word that struck me. Had he? Or had he been out at another business meeting?

Mum shrugged. "Either way, he's not here, Manny."

Dad exaggerated a similar shoulder gesture. "Then, my dear family, the old boy has probably fallen asleep somewhere in the sun. He'll turn up. How was work, Sharon? Any more gifts heading our way?"

She shook her head. I didn't dare explain my fear that the one he was expecting might not be coming either. She was unaware, of course, but I felt it.

She continued "No, Dad. She was in a funny mood. Those

soldiers were back, digging in that field behind the palace again. She was speaking to them and came back with a face set like fury."

Mum stopped her. Even now, she was still protective of us both. "You look worried, Shaz. Take your time."

"Mum, I can't bear that field after what I saw there. It still gives me nightmares. It's all too vivid."

"I'm not surprised, love." She opened her arms and Sharon went to her, sobbing.

When she'd dried her eyes, my sister looked around at us all and vocalised what we had been thinking. "What if Grandad's gone missing? I mean, has someone taken him? I'm scared."

Mum smiled weakly. "He'll be back, you'll see. It's like your dad thinks, he'll have dozed off."

"Mum, you don't think it's to do with what I told the queen. About him and the Lord. You don't think…"

I was trembling but before I could open my mouth, Dad was straight in. "Don't go there, Shaz, she's a good woman. Driven, I give you, but good. She wouldn't have any issue with an old codger. It's the intolerant leaders, the blinkered influencers, those so-called religious clowns who prevent others from the benefits of worshipping Baal that she's eliminated, and rightly so. Right, Ay?"

Mum's jaw dropped. "Erm, well, if you say so."

"Exactly. Jezebel's people are the true freedom fighters, giving our nation the choice we deserve. You've prayed to Baal, Ay, haven't you?"

Mum blew out her cheeks before expelling a breath and shrugging her shoulders. "I suppose so. If we are honest, we've all tried it when this awful famine has got to us. But I haven't made a habit of it."

I wasn't surprised at my mum's words, but I knew there was at least one exception in the family, one who would have given his life before accepting Baal. Grandad.

Sharon, though, wasn't listening to her mother. She took a deep breath and confronted her father. "I don't think Jezebel is right, Dad. You're wrong. You've become besotted by the queen." And with that, she let out a loud sob and headed to her room.

Dad sent her on the way. "Stupid girl! Grow up!"

Mum stopped me going after her, and in truth I was glad she did. My head was all over the place. I'd been bothered that I'd scuppered the hamper, but if Grandad had been taken, was that down to me too?

Then, I remembered Joel's last outburst at me, and I knew what had happened. He'd been re-programmed. Brainwashed. I hoped so in a way, surmising that he was not genuinely convicted in his own mind about the queen's aims and methods. Either way, he'd switched to her camp. He had dobbed Grandad in, presenting him as the puppet master in our hamper drama. And Jezebel had acted. My distaste for Joel was turning to hatred, and I was cut to the heart.

This was the young musician who was the love of my sister's life, at least in her opinion. The situation was dire. She wouldn't believe me if I told her. Love is blind, they say. She needed a decent man in her life right now, given the way our dad was treating her, and she had thought she had one. I needed her as my ally. This was no time to bring her crashing down with the truth. I had to carry the burden alone.

More immediately, Mum was ironic in her own distress. "Oh, well done, Manny. Thanks for all your help. Not!"

I experienced a further wave of hatred, this time for Dad, with his next outburst. "Shut your face, woman. Don't make me do something I'd regret."

No-one speaks to my mum like that, not even him. I resolved to never even pretend to pray to Baal with him again. I was starting to pile all my own guilt on top of the anger that I felt against my father. He'd lost the plot on this one. Family, food, hope, all gone. No solution. And no Grandad.

He grabbed his coat and shouted loudly so Shaz could hear him. "I'm not standing for this outrage. I'm going out to find my father. I'll bring him back and you will all apologise to me. No-one will eat in this house until you have retracted your words, all of you."

Mum couldn't hold back. I never thought I would hear her speak like this. "Not much of a threat, Manny, not in this famine!" Then she pulled back from the brink. "Go on, find him for all our sakes."

She placed her hands over her ears for the inevitable door slam. Then, he was gone.

Sharon and I were down early. Neither of us had slept well, probably for the same reason. I'd resumed ownership of my idiocy, and I resolved to tell the family - including my father - what I'd done, leaving out anything referencing Joel. But Dad had to be there.

My sister was first to get to my mother. "What time did Dad come back, Mum? Is Grandad in bed asleep?"

Mum sniffed. "He didn't find him. And your father was in such a rage that he spent the night in his barn. He came in for his breakfast ration and went straight out without a word."

Shaz really hadn't slept a wink. "It's all my fault, Mum. I told the queen about his beliefs and now she's taken him. That's what the soldiers were told to do. They've buried him in that field, I know it. My darling grandad."

Mum put her arm around her. "You don't know that, love. You're imagining things."

"Mum, I can't go to work today. She might have me seized too."

Mum spoke softly. "No, you're safe, Shaz. The queen's top make-up girl? You wouldn't be here today if she could afford to lose you. We'll have Grandad back today, and tonight we'll have the hamper, you'll see."

I knew we wouldn't be so lucky but restricted myself to a few words of support. Grandad would have been proud of me, I knew. "Shaz, Jezza will only be suspicious if you aren't there. Business as normal. Just keep your head down."

It worked. She smiled. "Head down? Not a good idea for anyone whose job it is to apply Jezza's make-up, Eran. You'll be suggesting that I ask her nicely if she knows where Grandad is next."

She reddened after realising her attempt at humour had failed. "Sorry. Sorry Grandad. We'll get you home soon."

Mum asked us if we would like to pray. For a moment, for the first time in my life, I was aware that there was only one God, the Lord, who could help. I prayed with an intensity I had never experienced before.

16

GUILTY

Shaz went to work, Dad stayed out, and I walked the fields to change my scenery. I hoped to find Grandad, maybe injured in one of the farm's dry ditches. I distracted myself by remembering the days when Dad drove me hard while he took time out. Bizarrely, I hankered for their return but suspected such hope was forlorn. Before I left, Mum was sporadically peering out to see if a certain gentle and lovely old man was on the horizon. I suspect that's what she did even when she was in the house alone. Neither of us saw any sign of him.

Later in the day, I walked the path he would have taken to meet Shaz. It was her usual finishing time, but she didn't appear. I can't describe the relief when I found her back home. Her Majesty Queen Jezebel appeared to have given her compassionate leave.

I had to ask. "Why? What reason did she give? Did you have a bit of a melt down?"

She hadn't. "No, she just sent for me after lunch and told me to take the afternoon off. I did what I was told. The other girls gave me very funny looks."

I would have too. First Grandad. Now, was Sharon being set up to disappear? It would have taken a full personality transplant to make Jezza's behaviour seem normal, but if anything, Sharon was more relaxed than when she'd left for the palace in the morning. And who had persuaded her to go in? Yours truly. If I wasn't guilty on the first count, I definitely was on this new one.

Dad did come back. He was exhausted and went straight to bed. Hamper Day was coming to a deeply unsatisfactory conclusion.

Did I hear a noise that night as I lay on my bed? I was restless. No-one else moved, so I stayed where I was. Morning came. I heard Mum go down, and she opened the door.

Moments later, we were all down. She'd done something she rarely did. She shouted. When we got there, she had five bags of fine fayre around her. There was no wicker basket, but who cared? We breakfasted like we hadn't done since before the famine. To three of the four of us, the Lord had answered our prayer.

When Dad slipped out for a moment, Mum whispered "He's fed Elijah, and now He's fed us."

I briefly chuckled to myself as I imagined the size of birds which would have been needed for this home delivery service, but Dad was back. His demeanour had returned to one we hadn't seen for a long time. He was acting the provider, the family hero. The irony didn't escape us. Then he saw Mum stowing a plate out of sight. "Secret rations, Ay? Are they for you when we're all out?"

Was he joking? I couldn't tell. He'd ruined the moment, though. Mum smiled gently. "One of the family's missing,

Manny. It's your dad's share for when he gets home. He's delivered the hamper as he promised."

Was it him? Where was he? Why hadn't he woken us? Why leave the bags outside? Why use bags in the first place? Yet again, the supply of questions exceeded the quantity of answers we had. Mum? She pondered whether the Lord had fixed the whole thing. Me? It was too incredible, but I wished it was true.

17

PLUMAGE

Those questions remained unanswered. After that first breakfast, Mum planned to make the food which we had left last for a week. I remembered my poison theory after we'd all eaten, so that wasn't Jezza's evil plot. Sharon worked her usual shifts and remained in the queen's favour. Dad's denials of the Lord became less vehement and less frequent, but Baal was still in his mindset. Me? I found any reason I could to wander the city streets as well as the farm to check anywhere Grandad could have been, but to no avail. After the novelty of that first breakfast, the taste of those luxuries seemed tainted, although no-one else complained.

Supplies dwindled as the week progressed. We resigned ourselves to resuming the boring diet we'd suffered since the famine began. Mum, though, was in good spirits, probably because she'd eaten properly, but I'm sure I heard her giving thanks for the provisions, and it wasn't to Baal. That's thanks in the face of forthcoming hunger. I didn't know what to make of it.

As the week drew to a close, my issues over that fateful

encounter with Joel, and the subsequent fallout, returned. Should I confess that dreadful day's events to the family? Were the food bags somehow a game changer? Grandad was still missing. How long would it be until that awful appendage 'presumed dead' would be added to his name?

Sharon's work had continued as before. She carried on dining on the queen's provision, as before, so no royal plumage was ruffled. Palace life went on as if nothing had happened.

But for me, Joel's treachery was a nagging and constant thought. Surely Sharon had to know that the man she loved was a collaborator. Was the turmoil of my guilt turning into a self-righteous need to protect my sister? How would she respond? And when was the time to do it? I had no answers.

Friday turned into Saturday. You may have picked up that my mother isn't one for shouting. It was exactly one week since the bags deposited by the mystery deliverer had been discovered, and once again, I was woken.

The ravens had returned. There were five more bags. And my mum was on top of the world.

I wasn't the only one whose slumbers had been broken by her cries of delight. Dad was already there ahead of me, and Sharon a few moments behind. Our parents were already exploring Mum's joyful find, and she knew the identity of the provider as she opened each bag.

"Manny, see what the Lord has done? He has answered our prayers. Just like He's taken care of Elijah!"

Dad pursed his lips. "I'd be careful, Ay. You're quoting a man who has been discredited. When the queen needed him, he did a runner. You can't trust a man like Elijah. He's a traitor to our glorious king and queen."

Mum, bless her, smiled as she irritated him. "So how do you explain the provision we've been granted? Baal? Really?"

"Baal's more a weather god, Ay. You know that. No, this is a coincidence. Or maybe someone at the palace is aware of my own loyalty and service to the king and queen and has seen fit to reward me."

Mum was on him. "Right. So why the secrecy? Why not a pomp-filled presentation ceremony in the presence of their majesties? Musicians, the works! Manny, they could even have sold tickets!"

I hadn't heard Mum like this before. Her sarcasm walloped my father in the stomach and he was, for the first time I could remember, utterly dumbstruck.

I threw in my shekel's worth. "Mum, you're forgetting. The music school's been shut down by the queen."

That was very unwise of me. Dad turned, furious. "Get out of here, Eran. Come back when you've learned to keep your mouth shut in front of your betters."

Wide-eyed, I instinctively reached for the door, but before I could open it, Mum put herself between us. "You stay right there, Eran. You are going nowhere."

The three of us were at an impasse. Then, to my surprise, Shaz's voice brought us to our senses. "I don't believe what I am seeing. There's been months and months of poor rations in this house, of Mum going hungry, and now we have all the food we could have dreamed of. And what's our response? We are at daggers drawn. Never mind beating each other up, and never mind which god you want to praise, get real. Get grateful."

My sister had grown up. I'd heard some assertiveness from

her previously, but she'd never spoken out before in this way. I was in awe. I swallowed my urge to ask her which god she would be lauding herself, but I guessed.

The situation thankfully melted into nothing. I mulled it over, of course. If she was advocating gratitude, did she know more than she was letting on? And did that place her in danger? Or was I overthinking it?

Grandad would have had advice for me, I knew. I recalled a story he told me when I was a little kid, about another palace. I remembered that according to him, the Lord placed a baby to grow up and be His presence there. He was called Moses. It was a story, like dads and mums tell their kids, and a good one. Did I believe it then? I was too young to do anything of that sort.

Now, though, I had to, if I was going to trust in the Lord's goodness for Grandad, wherever he was. We'd gone full circle, Grandad and me. Was the Lord speaking through reminding me of the Moses story? Was his presence in Pharoah's palace a metaphor for me? If Grandad was gone, was I to be the Lord's presence in our dysfunctional nation? Could I do that? Could I leave all my unanswered questions and concerns with the Lord? I decided to stay open to the idea.

18

PURIFICATION

There wasn't a day of the next three months that I didn't wrestle with that issue. He was dead, I knew that in my heart but couldn't acknowledge the fact. With every Saturday morning bringing more supplies, that childhood memory and Elijah's experiences dominated my mind. Mum looked so much better with the varied diet and was becoming her old self again.

Of course, I was desperate to see who or what was delivering those precious weekly bags, but such were the potential consequences for knowing the answer that I went with Sharon's view of simple gratitude. We all did. This was not a boat to be rocked.

I kept my eye on Shaz each day. She seemed blissfully unaware of the danger with which she was flirting. Going in her favour was her track record of apparently careless chatter with Jezebel, so the hamper pleading will have come across in the same way. I couldn't reveal Joel as a traitor to her yet, for fear of triggering all kinds of consequences from the fallout. But I did notice one minor thing. Our occasional habit of referring to the female monarch as Jezza stopped. Shaz seemed to be increasingly in the queen's good books, more than ever before. She, and she alone, was entrusted with the daily make-up and pampering. Shaz would relay some of their chats to us back home in the evening. It was all girls' talk, but even so, my dad hung on to every word. However, to me, it was apparent that my sister was becoming the queen's confidante.

It was the day after the latest bag drop off. The novelty of the provision had gone, and some of us were getting rather picky. My trust in the Lord must have imperceptibly grown in recent weeks, as I caught myself on the cusp of launching into a speech on how lucky we were. At that moment, in walked Shaz. Jezebel and she had been discussing Grandad.

Alarm bells rang in my head. Dad was wide-eyed, awaiting my sister's account. Mum looked down, as if she were fearing the worst.

"It was out of the blue. She asked how he was."

I was unable to hold back. "How he was? What do you mean? Did you tell her he was probably decomposing in an unmarked grave?"

There was a silence. After what seemed like an eternity, Mum's tone was soft. "Sharon, darling, Eran means well. What did you say to her?"

"Mum, I knew what to do. I got in that people of Grandad's age who followed the Lord were suffering. Not only from the effects of famine, but mentally, as they lived in fear of persecution."

Followed the Lord? In my head, that was us gone. A knock on the door in the night, wiped out by Jezebel's ruthless enforcers.

Mum smiled. "And how did she respond?"

"She told me those times were coming to an end. She claimed that the process of purification was over. The work was almost finished."

I needed to butt in, but Mum did it for me. "Did she say more about Grandad?"

"She did. That he could rest and be at peace."

I had to intervene. "Rest in peace, you mean?"

Sharon furrowed her brow. "No. If you'd let me finish my sentence, you wouldn't have interrupted me. Her words were that he could be at peace for the rest of his days."

"Did she mean he's alive?" I could barely get my question out.

"She smiled, if that helps. Then we moved on to talking new moisturisers, fashion and the likes, and her views of other people in the palace."

I hadn't finished. "The next ones she's going to bump off, Sharon?"

"No. I wish you'd stop interrupting me. She suggested that she'd been inspired by me and my caring attitude to Grandad. She said I'd influenced her in seeing the good in people, and that my friendship with her had changed things."

Dad, who'd said nothing, affixed the broadest grin across his features that I had ever seen since Jezebel's reign of terror had begun. Smug didn't cut it. This was self-righteousness, vanity and triumphalism.

I don't think Mum believed her ears, but she maintained a dignified smile. Me? This was another ploy, another trap, another annihilation strategy from an evil despot.

I glanced again at Mum. I knew what she was thinking

behind the smile, so back into my head came the question of the Lord. In my brain, if no-one else's, the evidence was mounting up that Jezebel's change of heart was wrought by His power. That woman could never have changed without supernatural interference. She was the personification of evil on earth, the devil incarnate. I wished the Lord would give me a sign, so I knew for sure. Or were the ravens really depositing our supplies? Despite sharing a little of Shaz's optimism, I still had more questions than answers.

Hunger issues apart, the next few weeks gave rise to a more relaxed feeling among the population. Even the royal guards were more at ease, and not just when they were told to stand that way. More people ventured out. Conversations were still cautious and short, but it did seem that Shaz had accurately read the queen's mind. The persecution was over.

Obadiah remained under the house arrest on which Jezebel had ultimately insisted, but one day, his guards didn't show up. No message, no conditions, nothing, so the poor man worked from home a little longer. Little by little, his confidence returned. He later explained that he had disguised his appearance and walked past the palace under the cover of darkness, the workplace where his oppressors had concocted their evil plans. No-one stopped him. He was spotted in the city square, his true identity revealed, reconnecting not only to surviving contacts from earlier days but new ones too, before resuming his former role, and requisite low profile, back in the palace.

There was still no sign of rain, so no work for me. I picked up the habit of visiting the city square, this time sitting with the elders, as Grandad had done. I had grown up. There was no sign of my father. He left the house before me every day, and I didn't have the foggiest where he went.

19

NONCHALANCE

A handful of traders and travellers began to join locals in the city square as the general sense of freedom improved. How odd that the absence of security guards should result in us all feeling safer, I thought to myself. Safety in numbers, I grant you, but these daily gatherings brought confidence. And on one such occasion, a traveller arrived, looking for Obadiah.

He was unlucky. The elusive Obadiah had passed through there the previous day, but not now. It was urgent, it appeared. I don't know why, but a consensus emerged among the regulars that I should act as the messenger. The traveller accepted, but only after asking for a quick individual character reference from a few of those around. He would not give me his name but spoke of urgency and secrecy. He escorted me around the corner to where I'd used to hang out as a kid, where no-one was in earshot. He gave me just four words for me to memorise.

As he left, continuing away from the square, I was overwhelmed by my foolishness in accepting the mission.

Why had I been chosen? Whose side was this stranger on? I hadn't even guessed what I might be getting into. But then, a spirit of assurance came from somewhere. A picture of Grandad appeared in my head, and he was smiling. He'd watched me play as a kid and seemed to be saying that if anyone could be a secret agent, it was me. The child in me had this. It was what I had trained for!

I'd no idea where Obadiah lived, of course. Spies don't ask questions, they either just know or they use strategies to find out. I resolved to wait till the great man did show up, and when he left, unobtrusively follow him to his home.

I adopted a gait of studied nonchalance which I felt was consistent with my new image, strolling back to the square where my fellow Jezreelites were still chatting.

One of them looked up and pointed. "His house is the fourth on the left past the big farmhouse."

My career in espionage went to the back burner. I'd forgotten that the traveller had asked for Obadiah. I slunk away sheepishly and for a reason I have never fathomed, I checked no-one was following me. Soon I was at the house. I surreptitiously looked left and right, checking for guards, but I was sure there were none. Obadiah's servant opened the door.

"Yes?"

"I have a message for Obadiah."

"That'll be Mr Obadiah to you."

How would a spy respond to that? I thought I knew. "Would you kindly enquire as to Mr Obadiah's availability for a brief word?" It didn't sound very spy-ish.

He looked down his nose. "He's not here."

Should I risk leaving a message? I knew it was urgent.

"And when might Mr Obadiah be back?"

"That depends. Mr Obadiah has business at the palace until late. Even he doesn't know when he'll have finished there."

"Will you give Mr Obadiah a message from me on his return? It's very short."

"I can't guarantee that. I am leaving his employment today. My replacement will be here anytime soon. When you arrived, I thought you might be him."

This was definitely not the response a spy should receive, I thought. I had much to work on.

"Is there a problem?" The voice came from behind me.

I turned round to see the great man frowning at me. Mr Obadiah was there. He waved his servant away. He had obviously taken time out from the palace.

I steadied myself and enunciated each word precisely. "He is returning tomorrow."

Mr Obadiah blinked. "What?"

I knew he had heard. "A message, erm, Sir."

"Oh, I see. Right. Who told you?"

I burbled. I wasn't cut out for this cloak and dagger stuff. "He was, erm, didn't say, erm, anonymous."

Was that a smile on Mr Obadiah's face? "A traveller?"

I took a deep breath. "I think so."

"Makes sense. If I were you, I'd tell no-one what you know. Better safe than securitised. God be with you."

With that, he went in and closed the door. Stunned, I wandered back to town. I had to pass through the square to get home, and did so, head bowed, studiously staring at my own feet.

"Eran?"

I had to look up. The speaker was the man who had sent me on the errand. "Elijah's on his way back, isn't he? We're guessing tomorrow."

I did what I learned as an older kid. I grunted. If you don't know what scurrying looks like, put yourself in my shoes right now, because that's just what I did. My dignity was scuppered. My bedroom was the only place to be.

The next day, I'd got over it. Back to the square I went. There was a buzz. I asked why.

"Word on the street is that Elijah is promising an end to the famine."

20

GROOMED

I wandered away. Not back home, but anywhere. I needed to think it through. Although their optimism was a tonic after such a long time, I began to question its authenticity. The word was encouraging on the surface, but I needed more. I longed for Grandad's advice. Anger flashed through my mind at whoever had taken him from me, but it was short-lived. I made no conscious decision to do this, but I found myself heading for Obadiah's home. When I reached the house, I trembled and dared not knock.

I shouldn't have worried. The door was held open by what I assumed was his new servant, but not for me to go in. The guy seemed familiar in some way, but I was looking for his master. Suddenly, Obadiah emerged. Did he notice me? Not at all. His clothing was smart, his hair well groomed. This was a man with a job to do, off somewhere important. His stride was purposeful and long. Feeling like a spy once again, I followed him. At a suitable distance, of course. His pace put me to shame, but I hung on until he made a turn towards the palace. I knew the lurking danger awaiting him within the walls and only hoped he did. I stopped still. Obadiah was approaching the gates.

In my mind's eye I saw Grandad's face and sensed his wisdom. He was indicating his approval, I was sure. I worried briefly that Obadiah was risking everything, maybe moving too boldly just days after returning to his place of work and, indeed, finding his freedom. Could this be another even more cunning trap? Was Jezebel luring him in and waiting to pounce? Was my destiny, my purpose, to try to stop him?

Of course it wasn't. Anyway, Jezebel would not need to trick him. She had had many chances to seize him, and still had that on a daily basis, but house arrest was as far as she could really go. There was an invisible protective ring around him which could only come from the same supernatural source as his courage. Grandad would have had no doubt.

My reverie ended abruptly when I was addressed by a female voice I knew very well.

"Eran! What are you doing here? You look like you are in a trance!"

"Shaz! Sorry, yes, I was dreaming. Shouldn't you be at work?"

"I just took a break. I'm doing a special treatment for the queen in an hour or so, it's quite intensive. The older she gets, the more work I have to do."

"Don't tell Dad that." I grinned. "Listen, take care today. Something's going on. I've just seen Obadiah going through the palace portals. He was dressed to the nines."

"I'll get back, then. I don't want to miss anything!" With those words, she was gone.

That evening, Shaz was late. After an hour, there was only Dad who wasn't worrying.

Our worries lasted a further hour. An audible sigh of relief greeted her arrival, looking exhausted.

Mum jumped to her feet. "Sharon, what happened today? Where have you been? Something's wrong, I fear."

Shaz glanced across at me. "Mum, I saw Eran near the palace after my break. He told me to be careful because he'd spotted Obadiah on his way in. Why Eran was there, I've no idea, but I'm glad he was."

Mum smiled at me. "Well done, Son. Sharon, did the queen make a scene with Obadiah? She's not exactly his number one fan."

"Not when she was with me, but the rest of the time she was totally out of her tree."

Dad tutted. "Sharon, show some respect for her Majesty, if you please. You owe her a great deal."

"Sorry Dad, it was scary. I walked past Obadiah after the queen summoned me for her treatment; he was as white as the palace walls. He was leaving."

"Did she talk to you about him?"

"She discusses everything with me, Dad. But he'd clearly upset her. Look, can I take a minute to just get changed before we go on? This is all so intense that I'm shaking."

She went up to her room. Mum whispered her instructions to my dad and me. "Keep cool, you two. Try and relax her when she comes back down. Don't make her anxious."

Dad snorted. A few minutes later, Shaz was back.

"Now where was I? Oh yes." She stared at Dad. "Her Majesty's cage had had a serious rattling when I went in. She was so snappy, it was like she bit my head off ten times."

I did my best to relax her. "Shaz, she could only do that once. Severed heads are terrible things for your balance."

That hit a nerve with my father. "You keep it shut, Son. This is no time for your quips."

I folded my arms. Grandad would have intervened, I knew, but me? I didn't know what to say. I felt like sulking.

My sister patted my shoulder as she spoke. "Without Eran today, I'd have run out of the room when she started."

Dad just couldn't stop himself. "And from there, straight into unemployment. Stupid girl."

I found my arm was around her. "Thank you, Shaz. I love you."

I felt her whole frame relax and she grinned. "That wasn't all. Jezebel calmed down, just like my father is going to do now, and began to discuss their meeting with me."

Wherever he was, Grandad's diplomacy had found a new platform at the family table. My sister was maturing into his role. Dad shuffled, as if to storm out, but was compelled to wait. It was not what he wanted to hear. Obadiah had requested an audience for Elijah the very next day. The rumour was true. He was returning to Jezreel.

Dad almost spat out each word in his next utterance. "She refused, I take it. Banned the man."

"No, Dad. She accepted. And do you know why? She told me that she valued her chats with me so much, especially those about Grandad, that she owed it to me to give Elijah at least a hearing."

I was surer than ever that this was a trap. Elijah was the queen's sworn enemy.

Mum just nodded. "You still haven't told us why you were late."

"She talked for ages, of course, about all the issues it had raised. She asked to meet Grandad. She obviously doesn't know he's been killed."

"We don't know for sure, Shaz. Look, either Jezebel's grip on reality is loosening, or she's tricking you into saying stuff you don't want to be telling her about our family. Don't be playing with fire. I'd back off, if I were you."

Hypocrisy? Probably. My imagined spy mission suddenly framed me as a rebel, and my journey towards accepting the Lord didn't help. At least I was protecting Shaz.

Dad? I suppose he saw that the world he had supported so mindlessly was slipping from his control. His daughter was no longer his little girl, and I knew that my actions were those of adulthood too. He snorted fiercely, slapped the table firmly with his hand, then went out grumpily into the darkness.

21

DOOMED

I didn't sleep that night. Thoughts stormed around my brain. I knew more than my father and sensed acutely the responsibility which had been placed upon me. Was it by the Lord? It hit me with the power of a lightning strike that I hadn't realised the depth of the impossible position which poor Sharon was in. If the queen's regime was heading to its end, she would be seen as one of her allies. If Jezebel was playing games, she would dispose of Sharon as soon as she had no further use for her. Why do things always seem worse during the night? This adult world of intrigue which I had romanticised in my mind was mucky. I just wanted to be a kid again.

Sharon seemed oblivious to it all. I still hadn't told her the truth about Joel. However, she did not need to know my concerns as she plodded off to the palace the next morning. But when she returned, it was with a bombshell.

"Good day at the office, Shaz?" My question was in all innocence.

"It was until Elijah showed up."

Everyone stopped. Dad pretended to be pre-occupied with staring at his bowl, but Mum and I were agog.

"He met Jezebel?" Mum was incredulous. "It actually happened?"

"Well, I did tell you she would. Mum."

Mum echoed my thoughts from the day before. "It can't have been easy. Aren't they sworn enemies?"

"They are. There was a lot of shouting, all from her. We heard her from two rooms away. We couldn't hear him, he was so calm, superficially at least. I only found out a few minutes later how he managed to stay there, when she sent for me. Elijah had gone by then."

"I take it this wasn't for a facial, Shaz. What happened when you went into the royal presence?" Dad looked at me disapprovingly as I spoke but thankfully kept his counsel.

"First of all, I had to calm her down. She was furious. Not with me, you know, just the way things were."

Dad did speak. "I'm sure her Majesty controlled her own temper without help from a make-up girl."

Mum held up her hand. "You weren't there, Manny. Sharon was. Give her some credit for once."

He was lost for words. Did he apologise? Of course not. But Mum had silenced him in a way I had never seen before, and I was amazed. I asked Sharon to carry on, and as I did so, I realised I was stepping into the shoes my father was choosing not to wear.

"Ok, so I calmed her down." Shaz looked at Dad. He avoided her gaze. "She told me that she was facing a crisis. Elijah had been promising an end to the famine. It was exactly what people needed to hear. Word was flying around the city, and he was gaining hundreds of followers by the minute."

"Spell it out for us, Sharon. Why did she perceive that as a problem?" Mum was trying to comprehend Jezebel's mindset.

"Mum, she needs the famine to end as much as everyone else. Even those imported palace food supplies have begun to dwindle. When you've had what she's had, you always want more, not less. Her staff are grumbling about what they get to eat there, and it's beginning to get to her."

I sensed that there was more. "She would have liked to be the announcer of the good news, but Elijah has beaten her to it. Right?"

"Right, Eran. But he is claiming that he is bringing a message from the Lord. He told Elijah that He was ending the drought."

I got it. "She was presuming Baal would do that. He's the local weather god, remember."

"Yes, she's backed a few idols in her time, but he's her top god. Baal is her justification for the way she wields power. If Baal fails, her whole credibility is gone. If that happens, the regime may be doomed."

"She told you all this, yes?" Dad's intervention risked his wife's newly discovered wrath. She nodded her approval.

Sharon relaxed at the parental de-escalation. "Yes, Dad, and more. She felt that Elijah had got her in a corner."

"Off with his head, I'd say." Dad grinned, but it wasn't funny.

"Seriously, Dad, she's too late. The movement against her would escalate beyond control. It's bad enough now, as she sees it."

"So, what's our dear queen going to do?" I couldn't see her way out.

"She's agreed to a showdown. It's like Jezebel versus Elijah."

Mum looked pensive. "Baal versus the Lord, you mean. She's playing with fire. It looks to me like there's only one possible winner there."

In my heart, I knew she was right. Two days later, the politics of it all had begun. Sharon's return from work was never so eagerly anticipated.

"So, there's going to be a grand assembly. A huge audience. All the Baal teachers are being called together. And community leaders from our whole nation. A parliament. And I might be there too."

Dad was more careful with his words this time. "Love you as we do, Shaz, you're hardly a representative of the people. No chance."

"That's exactly where you are wrong. The queen has already asked me to accompany her."

"Asked? Royalty don't ask. They command. They order. They demand. They require." Dad was back on his pro-monarchy stand.

Mum exhaled. "Manny, if Sharon says she's been asked, that's what's happened. Don't let your lack of ability in maintaining relationships colour the real picture of your daughter's achievements."

Sharon smirked. "There's a bit more to it than that, Mum. Her public face will need a scrub up. And I'm her girl."

I wanted the details. "Where's this going to happen, Shaz?"

She laughed. "Where do you think?"

Dad was clear. "This is no time for guessing games, Sharon. Show respect. There is nothing funny about Queen Jezebel."

I chimed in. "You're right there, Dad. It's pretty tragic, if only you would look."

Before he could escalate my comment to another full-blown row, Shaz shrugged her shoulders dramatically. "You wouldn't have guessed anyway, none of you. It's at the top of Mount Carmel."

"Where? What? You can't ask her Majesty to ascend so high just for an event. There's rough terrain to cover on the way up."

I couldn't resist. "Come on Dad, she'd look stunning! Top quality make-up by Sharon and looking gorgeous in a pair of mountain shorts and hiking boots!"

Dad shook his head in total disbelief. "What's going to happen up there? A whole lot of talking?"

It was Shaz's turn to shake her head. "No. It's a showdown."

This sounded good. "Whose idea was the venue, Shaz?"

"Elijah's. She is so confident in Baal that she offered him anywhere, expecting him to decline. But he didn't. He chose Mount Carmel."

"He went for the moral higher ground, then."

Mum missed my humour as her brow furrowed. "Wasn't there an altar to the Lord up there at one time?"

Neither Sharon nor I knew, to our shame. Dad did, but he wasn't for mentioning it.

He did know one thing. "It's become the haunt of robbers and bandits. There's plenty of cover there, and caves too. It's an odd choice, but then this Elijah bloke is an odd sort of chap."

Mum sniffed. "Many people say that he's a man of principle, if that's what you mean. Probably more than that."

I agreed. "Badly treated, too." I didn't say by whom. "He'll have the rain up his sleeve too."

Mum laughed. "Not a helpful image, Eran, but there is a spirituality about him, for sure."

I came back with a question. "Are you saying that Elijah would reign with rain if he could rein in the queen's spirits?"

Mum got it this time, with a sharp riposte. It was great to see her so bright. "No, but Jezebel might resort to her crystal Baal."

Dad winced. I glanced at my sister. "When's the showdown happening, Shaz?"

It was imminent. "It's on Friday. We leave the palace tomorrow. I'll be gone a couple of days."

22

PIE

Dad was definitely playing it cool. Friday came and Friday went. Shaz returned the following evening, and he was bursting to quiz her on the outcome. Mum hugged her. Dad didn't, but he was swift off the mark with his interrogation. And I was keen to take some of the wind out of his sails.

"What happened, Sharon? Was it all talking?"

"Not exactly, Dad. All the great and the good were there. Monarchists, mostly."

"Right. Followers of Baal."

"Yes, and they were pretty outspoken at first. Like loud, you know."

"Did the queen encourage them?"

"Not then, Dad. She didn't show up. Ahab did."

I had to ask. "Where was she?"

"Back in the palace. We'd already set off. One of the palace staff told us that Ahab had decided it was time he took over the whole unseemly business."

Really? I had to follow that one up. "Shaz, that wouldn't have pleased the queen, would it?"

"Certainly not. She was awaiting her carriage at the time. He approached her and gestured to her to go back indoors. She was not a happy monarch."

Dad was nonplussed for a moment. "What? He's only been interested in the military in the past. Why would a comedy show bother him?"

Sharon shrugged her shoulders. "Apparently one of the palace staff caught the king's attention and apprised him of the issues at stake."

"That was brave. Wait a moment, how did he know about what was going on anyway?"

"Dad, I don't know. But I can tell you that this guy was sure of his information. Ahab's no fool. He knows a threat to his kingdom when he hears one."

Dad tried to move the conversation on. "Either way, king or queen, I assume royalty ruled the roost and Elijah ate a large portion of humble pie."

"Not exactly, Dad. It wasn't like that. Two bulls were selected, you know, because they can be a symbol of Baal. They were to be sacrificed in front of all the assembly, and there were a great many people there."

I jumped in. "No pie at all, Dad. Just bull. I'm relieved they weren't young ones. Baal and a load of b…"

I stopped in my tracks as his features assumed an unmerited expression, a kind of metaphysical altitude, before raising his voice. "You dare, Eran. You just dare. I will not tolerate such language in this house." He shifted his gaze uncomfortably before lowering his tone. "Sharon, what happened next?"

She suppressed a snigger. He wasn't fazing her anymore. "It was trial by fire. The first animal was cut up by the leaders of the Baal faction. It was agreed that they would then prove their god's power by calling on him to set fire to the sacrificial meat."

Dad was still perplexed. "Elijah had set the rules, right? How did Ahab ever permit such a contest?"

Sharon corrected her father. "He didn't. By the time he got involved, it was all agreed. This was Jezebel's doing. Once she had accepted the challenge, that was it. Ahab would have lost all respect if he'd backed off in any way."

Mum nodded. "That makes sense, Sharon. Did you witness what ensued?"

"I did, Mum. They made fools of themselves. In full sight of everyone, they called out to Baal. No result, not even a flicker of a flame. They begged Baal to light up their day literally, but no response came. Next, they implored him. Nothing happened. So, they held a huddle. A big one."

"That would have made no difference, I guess." Mum was clear.

"None whatsoever. All this took the whole of the morning. The crowd had become restless, so these prophets resorted to a few dance steps to attract Baal's attention, but I'll be honest, their moves weren't great. They kept shouting until Elijah got involved with proceedings."

Dad was back in. "He's got a nerve."

"Not really. He made a few suggestions, like Baal was having forty winks, taking a few moments of reflection, too occupied with other followers to have time for them, and finally away on his holidays."

"That would not have gone down well, Sharon." Dad shook his head.

"It was worse than that. They turned on themselves. I

thought they had concluded that they needed a different type of sacrifice to get Baal involved, so started slashing themselves with their swords. However, one of my colleagues suggested that there wasn't much hope for them by this stage, as they had failed the queen and even the king, so they probably wouldn't have seen the next morning in one piece anyway. Elijah gave them all day to fulfil their aims and their failure was total."

"That made difficult viewing for the crowd, I guess." Mum was stating the obvious.

"Yes, but eventually it was Elijah's turn. The time for the evening sacrifice had arrived. That was when things changed. Elijah called the people to move closer so they could see everything he did, right by the old altar from when our people all followed the Lord. Elijah fixed it up as it had been damaged. He took a stone for each of our twelve tribes and made a new table with them and dug a trench round it."

Dad affected a yawn. "You'd think they'd have gone home if he did all that. Weren't they bored? Watching one man lift a few rocks and then do a bit of digging doesn't constitute great entertainment in my book."

"Believe me, Dad, they were entranced. They knew the symbolism alright. He didn't do ten of the stones, and then a separate two. This was about reunification. So, all eyes were on Elijah. The warm-up act hadn't delivered any sense of theatre to support Ahab's regime. The royal reliance on Baal was flaking in front of their eyes. And a one-man show was about to rock the regal boat."

Mum grinned. "Come on, Sharon, don't spin it out. What did Elijah do?"

"Mum, he put the firewood onto his construction, then spread the pieces of the sacrificial animal on it."

"Don't tell me, the Lord set them on fire, and everyone cheered."

"Steady on, Mum. Three times, Elijah sent for four large water containers. He poured the liquid all over the meat and the wood until they were totally soaked. That created a sense of anticipation."

Mum nodded. "Were the people good at maths, Sharon?"

She paused. "What do you mean?"

"Four threes are twelve, love. There was symbolism in Elijah's work."

"At that precise point, they were watching him like they viewed a magician, trying to catch him out in his tricks. Maybe they realised later."

"How did it end?"

"Elijah prayed to the Lord for all the people. His prayer was asking Him to speak into their hearts to turn them back to Himself. Suddenly, fire broke out, but not normal fire. It burned the animal he'd sacrificed, but all the wood was gone."

Dad had been waiting for an opportunity to derail the account, and here it was. "How's that not normal, Sharon? You've let your imagination run wild."

"You're wrong, Dad. First, it was all soaking wet. Secondly, the stones were burned away along with the soil beneath, and thirdly, the flames dried out the trench which had been full of water. This was no magic trick. This was the hand of the Lord. He didn't play with fire. He owned it."

Mum looked like she was on the point of tears, like she'd realised the error of some of her wanderings. I just froze, open-mouthed. Dad, though, was still looking for mitigation. "Did Ahab take control at this point, Sharon? Dismiss the crowd, send them home?"

"It wasn't the king who addressed them, Dad. It was Elijah. He told them to turn on the Baalite so-called prophets who were watching on fearfully as all this unfolded, licking their wounds. The few who were able legged it, only to be pursued and caught by the angry spectators, whilst the rest were marched down Mount Carmel. A few of us palace staff went too, although a couple stayed on at the top with Ahab, too stunned to know what the best thing was to do. I'm glad they did."

"Why?" I knew there had to be a reason.

"Let me finish, Eran." Sharon's smile caught me off guard, especially in the light of her next words. "The whole lot of them were put to death, whilst the people repented and accepted the Lord as their one true God."

"Weren't you shocked?" I felt for the poor girl.

She seemed strangely immune. "No. The sense of the Lord's presence filled me as it did everyone who saw it. It was the Lord who was taking their lives. It was a proper act of purification." She saw my face. "I'm more than fine, Eran. I know it sounds incredible, but righteousness ruled. I witnessed direct intervention from Yahweh."

Dad had one final question. "Is Ahab still alive?"

Sharon nodded. "Elijah sent him off to go for some food and drink and told him he thought he heard the sound of rain."

"What?" Dad was utterly bemused. "Elijah commanded the king to take time out for a meal break?"

"This is the point, Dad. It was Elijah's voice, but the Lord was speaking. The Lord was taking back His own people. He is their true king."

"Hang on, did the rain we've just had start before all this excitement?" Dad was struggling to justify his own mindset.

"Oh, certainly not. Elijah's a fit guy. He went straight back up to the top of Mount Carmel, past the shelter where Ahab was eating and drinking. Elijah went back to pray, to seek the Lord. He got down on his knees, my colleagues from up there told me afterwards, then, apparently, he seemed to send a chap off a few times to check if there was a raincloud heading his way. They told me that it worked the seventh time, and the same chap was despatched to see Ahab and get him into his chariot and on his way down the mountain before the route became impassable through flooding."

"That's when the rains came?" Mum's question was really more of a statement, but Shaz affirmed it anyway. "Yes. The next arrival from the summit which we at the bottom of the mountain spotted was not Ahab in whatever remained of his glory, but Elijah, who'd outrun the procession. He'd not only won the showdown but got back to Jezreel before Ahab. Victory must have tasted sweet."

Mum looked at her. "I don't suppose he saw it that way, Shaz, but yes, what a day!"

Dad had spotted the issue. "Meanwhile, Queen Jezebel was fuming. Not only was she enraged at her husband's behaviour and the way it had all unfolded, but she's going to want to have Elijah for toast. Believe me, this is not the end. Sharon, be very careful if our queen calls for your services at the palace. What you have seen might set her against you as well. Baal may be deflated, but is he out?"

23

HAYSTACK

That night, I pondered my parents' words. The rain reassured me. Dad would have me back in the fields as soon as the celebrations were over. Whilst he would drive me hard, I rejoiced in the arrival of a new normal.

Months would need to pass before that happy state was fully restored, however. The greyness of the figurative, depression-filled clouds of famine repercussion was slowly replaced with the real rain-bearing ones which, oddly, were joyfully darker.

But I digress. Were Mum and Dad both right? Dad's assessment of punishment to be visited on Elijah, and Mum's question over the same man's speed to get back to Jezreel before Ahab?

Mum made Sharon promise to keep a low profile at the palace before she left for work. I expect it made Mum feel better, but Shaz knew she was at Jezebel's beck and call, so it wasn't going to be easy. Later, I went up to the square to gauge the atmosphere.

It was one of unease. Rumours were rife of a royal row and

rift of epic proportions, and a squad of soldiers despatched to detain Elijah. I couldn't confirm the former, but the latter was evidenced by military presence in various parts of our city. Elijah was a wanted man. Dad was right.

Despite my father's attempts to appear aloof from the situation, we were all anxious to see Sharon coming down the track around the usual time. Our fears were relieved, and this time, no-one needed to ask her anything. Her account of the day poured from her lips as soon as she got home, and her voice was not as calm nor her thinking as mature as it had lately become. Why? That soon became apparent.

"The shouting was atrocious. Jezebel let fly at Ahab so loudly, the whole palace could hear. She humiliated and crushed him. The debacle of the previous day was dissected, and Ahab must have feared the same fate. Every time he tried to answer, she just bellowed even louder. Then she demanded Elijah's head. Talk about shooting the messenger! Jezebel has ordered his death."

Mum put her hand on Shaz's shoulder. "That must be so distressing for you, my dear."

"Mum, it's so wrong. He was one against hundreds yesterday and he clearly won."

"Yes, Shaz. Unfortunately for Ahab, the crowd switched to Elijah's side, leaving Ahab on his own. His impotence against Elijah's firmness of faith in the Lord left him isolated. It wasn't even the king who ordered the death of the Baalite prophets. That was Elijah too."

Shaz paused a moment. "Erm, yes, I guess so. The thing is, she's taken Ahab out of the equation by giving the order to the military for Elijah's execution within 24 hours."

Mum inhaled sharply. "That won't solve anything. Did she summon you today, or leave you in peace?"

"Later on, yes, she sent for me. She'd calmed down a bit. She needed more than a few touches on her make-up, and I could tell she'd been crying. I spoke soothingly and stroked her hair as she relaxed a little more."

"She really does trust you, Sharon." Mum was equally soothing for her daughter.

"What did she tell you?" My impatience had the better of me.

"She was still angry at her husband."

Dad frowned. "You mean our esteemed king. Sharon. This is no time for disrespect."

"I wasn't disrespecting anyone, Dad. Jezebel felt the carpet had been totally whisked from under her feet. Our esteemed king had trampled over her feelings like a live one of Baal's bulls in a palace dining room. He'd left her in charge of running the show whilst he spent his days drinking with the macho men who dress up and march around as soldiers, then suddenly, he panics and supervenes. I told her I understood."

"I don't like your tone, Sharon."

"Dad, you don't get it. It was Ahab who had shown no sensitivity. I'm just the reporter."

Dad sniffed. "Ok that explains the row they had. Any couple would have that. Being monarchs doesn't prevent them having a bit of a barney every now and again."

"I suppose not. It became quickly apparent that she was apportioning far more blame to Elijah for ordering the death of her favourite prophets."

I got involved. "The ones who had failed? That was a bit irrational, wasn't it?"

"Like I say, Eran, I'm telling you what happened, not giving you my opinions."

"So, it's true, she's put a contract out for Elijah's head?"

"Yes. She felt that Baal would require that."

"Had they brought Elijah in by the time you left?"

"No. He was ahead of the game. That's what added fuel to the fire."

I couldn't resist it. "Not a helpful image, Shaz. The Lord doesn't require any additives. He is fire. So how was Elijah one step ahead of her Majesty?"

"It wasn't one step. It was lots of them. Elijah didn't stop running when he got to Jezreel. That's why he outsprinted the king's chariot. And he ran for six miles."

"That's hard to believe, Shaz. Sprinting is what you do for short distances, not six miles."

Mum stepped in with a level of confidence in her voice which I hadn't heard for years. "Not where the Lord is concerned. If you believe He brought fire to wet firewood and fresh raw meat, plus rain to the land, moving Elijah at pace is small beer. No wonder Jezebel is feeling wounded. Do the maths. She's lost all her Baalite teachers, leaders and spokespersons as well as hundreds of followers."

I piped up. "Yes, it isn't looking good, the prophet and loss account."

Mum laughed, Shaz grinned. Dad glowered at me before speaking. "Do they know Elijah's location, Sharon?"

"No, it all happened too quickly. He disappeared into the desert."

Mum verbalised my thinking. "That's tough, He's saved us all, and he pays the price. He's gone where there's no food or drink while we prepare to celebrate the new life brought by the rain. Are they sure he's alone, Sharon?"

"The queen didn't know. I spoke to one of the guards whose information was that they followed a lead which suggested that one of his followers insisted on going with him, but they found neither him nor his supporter. It was like looking for two needles in a mega haystack."

"In that case, I'm sure that Yahweh will take care of his needs. He had done the Lord's work in the face of the enemy."

I indicated my agreement. "There's a redundant flock of ravens all fed and ready to fly. Elijah will be protected."

24

INVASION

The next six months was a time of easing. The rains came when they should, and life returned to normal. Did all the people turn their backs on Baal? Of course they did, for the first couple of weeks.

Mum monitored the strategy as it evolved from the palace officials. They set out to cancel Elijah. His character was called into question. His actions were reduced to self-interest. The narrative of his escape was amended. According to the powers that were, Elijah was seeking to overthrow the regime and take power. He had run off in fear when Ahab followed him in the chariot.

It didn't make sense, of course, to those of us who understood the struggle on a different level. Speaking of which, Baal was reinstated. Elijah had done the trick with the fire, but Baal had heard the cries of his prophets and took a bit longer than we were all expecting to get the rain back on the crops. The city and the nation slipped reluctantly back into a routine which was similar to the old days, but with a renewed sense of political oppression. There was an acceptance that Elijah's commendable efforts had been to no avail.

Dad was ebullient, of course. Sharon settled back well into routine, and I was busy on the farm. Mum kept house and we all fed well.

Then came a change of tune from the royal regime. Our nation, our culture, our lifestyle, all was under threat from a neighbouring country, Aram. Sure enough, the military was despatched as news of an invasion by their forces reached Jezreel.

The mood altered. For Ahab, it was what he lived for. For Jezebel, there was more power to be seized in her husband's absence. For our family, Sharon seemed to be staying later and later at work, which we put down to her expanding role as Jezebel's closest advisor.

Two days later, there was an early morning knock at our door. Mum got there first. She found two figures on the doorstep, one a soldier and the other little more than skin on bones, an old man with head bowed, leaning on the arm of his escort.

Mum's sharp intake of breath was audible upstairs. I hurried down. "Help him in, Eran. Get a chair and some water." She was shaking.

I did as she had bid me. I took his arm and knew immediately who it was. He tried to squeeze my hand. He felt his way into the house with his other hand and I steered him to the chair I had pulled out in readiness. He sipped the water Mum put to his lips. Then, briefly, he smiled. Grandad was home.

Dad and Shaz had sensed our shock. My sister's tears were

unceasing as she surveyed this shadow, this wreck of a man who had meant so much to us. She kissed his head and stroked his shoulders. When he raised his head, we noticed his eyes were fixed and looking upwards. Grandad was blind.

Mum warmed him some soup. He swallowed a couple of mouthfuls before a raking cough brought it back up. He was never to shake it off.

Dad took over. He sent Shaz to prepare his old bedroom, then motioned to me to help take him there. We carried him painstakingly before laying him on his mattress.

Shaz had to go to work. I sensed my father was about to tell her to thank the queen, but even he was struggling with his emotions. The man we thought was dead was alive, if barely so.

Our farmwork wouldn't wait either. Mum told us to go. No-one could take better care of Grandad, I thought, than my mum. And for a whole week, she nursed him. He slept a great deal, often with one of us holding his hand, but little by little, he recovered something of his former self.

I can't recall which day he began to speak with any coherence, but the gamut of emotions we had experienced was stretched further as so many questions arose.

Why now? Why return him from captivity? How was he blinded? Why wasn't he killed? Why hurt an innocent old man?

It was a different quest which was occupying Jezebel and Shaz. The former's spy network reported Elijah somewhere in the vicinity of Mount Horeb, aka Sinai. The ravens must have done their delivery job to get him there, I thought, and Horeb was the place where Moses met with the Lord when he gave him the ten commandments. It's a holy place in our tradition.

Shaz got this info from the queen. What she forgot to add was that a storm of supernatural proportions preceded Elijah's arrival, followed by an earthquake. Then fire. In the city square, the regulars were sure of this, almost as if they too had an informant. And the fire was self-extinguishing, just like on Mount Carmel. Guess what came next? A voice from heaven, giving the great man more tasks elsewhere. Elijah was back on the road.

I was stunned. Our God, as I now knew Him, was awesome. The man who had pointed me to Obadiah's house took me to one side once more, to the familiar spot. He had more detail. Elijah's latest remit was to line up a couple of new kings in preparation for coming vacancies. I asked where the opportunities were, and he told me a man called Hazael would be reigning in Aram, whilst Jehu would be the new King of Israel. The man spoke with a rare authority.

Then he shook his head. I looked at him, entranced. He shrugged his shoulders. "Elijah didn't carry out his tasks."

"Why not?"

He didn't know why not but told me Elijah had taken on an apprentice. "He's been through the mill more than once. The young fellow is called Elisha, and we may well see him completing the Lord's tasks."

I felt bewildered. Elijah had become my hero, and I wanted better from him. Before I could ask that of my informant, he gave me a solemn warning.

"My friend, you remember the famine?"

That struck me as a stupid question. "Of course. We all do."

"What was that? I don't mean a lack of food."

I thought swiftly and came up with a phrasing Mum had used. "The Lord's punishment for His people after they rebelled against Him."

He nodded. "That's right. And what has happened since the rains returned?"

I knew this one immediately. "They've slipped back into their old ways. Ahab and Jezebel too."

"Yes, the Lord has given His people, including the royals, every opportunity to turn back to Him. They haven't taken it, by and large. So, what comes now? Our nation gets what's due to them."

His words made sense. I pointed to the sky. "He's even given signs. He's shown His power. I guess the coming punishment is totally deserved."

My collocutor responded in hushed tones. "It looks to me that the nation will be punished by outside forces. If Hazael becomes King of Aram, he won't spare our people. And Jehu's a bad egg too, if what I hear is right. It seems to me that the Lord is unstoppable. Whatever happens, His purposes will be fulfilled. Jezebel and her evil plans have escalated matters. We are seeing our God moving to save His people. We live in tempestuous times."

I had to ask. "Are you saying that the Lord will use those we would describe as evil to deliver punishment on His own people?"

He stroked his chin. "Let's look at it another way. He has given the nation a clear choice and His option so far has been rejected. He has shown extraordinary patience but that will not last forever."

25

VEGETATION

Shaz continued to enjoy the queen's favour for many months. Grandad's convalescence was slow and at times excruciatingly painful, but he adjusted to his disability and we did too.

Then with the news that our forces had defeated those of Aram came a surge in Jezebel's level of ebullience to one which we had not seen before.

"She was on one today alright." Shaz was back, late as per usual.

Grandad, Mum and I were in the kitchen with her. Mum went first. "What's she on about this time?"

Sharon smirked. "You won't believe this one. It's vegetables."

I wasn't sure I'd heard her right. "Did you say vegetables? Really? One minute she's issuing death threats and the next she's into market gardening. That woman's unstable."

Grandad nodded. He still had a spark of humour. "Cool as a cucumber with it."

"As a what?" I hadn't a clue what he was talking about.

Shaz helped me out. "Something they buy in for the palace. From abroad. They're quite exotic."

There hadn't been anything of that name in the food bags. We moved on. Shaz took up the narrative.

"During the famine, royal dining depended on other countries selling produce to the palace kitchens. Now the war with Aram is won, she's getting into reducing dependence on external sources. She wants to grow her own."

Mum smiled. "And share the secrets with our own farmers. Wonderful idea if the conditions suit it."

Sharon frowned. "Not the way she was talking today, Mum. It's largely for herself."

It was my turn to frown. "Even Jezebel can't eat her body weight in veg, Shaz. I know the Lord has manifested in a great wind, but this is taking things to the extreme."

"What's my job with her Majesty?" Her question was rhetorical. "Vegetable matter is a constituent part of make-up. Vegetation, flowers and all that, puts the purr into perfume. Culinary concerns are a by-product, nothing more. She's getting older. Her complexion needs are changing."

"Maybe we can oversee the production on our farm here, Sharon. Your father would love to supply the queen with what she needs." Mum was serious.

"That's the other problem. She wants to keep it in the palace grounds. The issue is where. There's no space for horticulture on the site, so she's spotted the next best thing. A field she can survey from her own bedroom."

"Where are we talking, Sharon?" Mum was not a regular around the palace grounds. "Is it near Naboth's vineyard?"

Shaz shook her head. "No, Mum, it's not near it. It is

Naboth's vineyard. That's the problem."

Grandad raised his head. "He's an oldie now, but his wine is the finest in the kingdom. Jezebel knows that, because in the palace, they drink lots of it."

Shaz smiled. "It's down to the quality of the soil. Her own needs trump everyone else's."

Grandad was taking it all in. "Will Naboth sell?"

There was something melancholy about Sharon's reply. "Ahab has approached him. He doesn't want the neighbours upset, and he's rather partial to Naboth's recent vintages. The queen doesn't give a hoot."

I stepped in as Grandad was fumbling for words. "Was Naboth reasonable?" Sharon grimaced. "Yes. He clarified that the land had been in his family for generations, and he'd be very obliged if the king left him to his labours." I was glad Dad wasn't with us.

Mum followed it up. "How did that go down?"

Sharon shrugged. "I'm reading between the queen's words, to mix a metaphor. I suspect that Ahab was fine, although he knew he'd be getting another mouthful of choice language from his wife. I gather he was depressed but accepted he'd done what he could."

"And Jezebel took it like a lamb, I suppose." Irony and Mum were a rare but powerful combo.

"The queen has told me that she ordered him to man up. She's setting up a kangaroo court a week today and Naboth will be tried for treason on two counts. That's one against the Lord as well as the other against the king."

Mum's eyes sparkled. "So, she's accepted that the Lord is God? That's the only logical conclusion."

Shaz wagged her finger from side to side purposefully. "No, she's using the Lord to achieve her selfish demands. We'll wait and see, of course, but I don't think it's going to be good. The Lord's not going to be as charitable as she is gambling on."

Jezreel awoke to the day of the trial with consternation. Naboth was a respected winemaker whose produce had been celebrated by generations of his family before him. In the square, there was a consensus that King Ahab would see common sense prevail.

I wasn't so sure. Mum expected no more than a charade. "The procedure means sending Obadiah with instructions to put before the city council. The reality is that they don't wield much clout. The king just over-rides them if he feels that way out. I don't really know why he is bothering this time."

Dad appeared as she finished speaking. "Procedural issues are important. The king will do all required of him, you can be sure of that."

I wasn't. This was not a military matter. Custom and practice was now that this fell under the jurisdiction of the queen who ran everything but the army. This was a struggle between good and evil, and I knew which side I was on.

As the day progressed, rumours ran wild over the forging of trial documents. Some were saying that Jezebel was in the power of the devil. Was our proud warrior-king about to be defeated by his own wife? We feared for Naboth.

In the fields that afternoon, I decided to challenge my father when he returned from his old habit of absenting himself for a meeting in the city. I asked him why Ahab was not a strong ruler.

As soon as I closed my mouth, I regretted my words. I needn't have worried at all, though. Dad was surprisingly forthcoming.

"Time for a lesson on life, Son. Ahab's a great leader on the field of battle, but like many before him, he's a man. He's been overwhelmed by this beautiful woman. At times, he can't see past her."

"Dad, does he have the courage to put her in her place?"

Dad sighed dramatically. His answer was uncharacteristic and unexpected. "Away from the army, he avoids a dog fight at all costs. Anything for a quiet life."

"They say his rewards come in bed. Is that right?"

I was staggered that Dad deigned to answer my questions. Was it because he and I were alone?

"You're a man now, Eran. We men should never speculate inappropriately about the private life of any couple, and our gracious royal family is no exception. You will realise for yourself soon that sex is powerful. It's a hold some women can take over their men. Watch out for that, my boy."

Shaz would never be like that, I thought, but whilst he was like this, I could ask him about the risks she might be taking daily. I'd never talked to her as I once wanted to, never telling her what I knew about Joel, but now I could get some reassurance. Or not.

I took a deep one and went for it. "Some people are convinced that Queen Jezebel is in the power of Satan. Your daughter, my sister, keeps her looking great for him. How should we feel about that? And isn't she therefore in great danger?"

He put his hand on my shoulder for the first time in years.

"Leave that to me, Eran. You're making a lot of assumptions there. There are times in life when your experience and wisdom are less comprehensive than your elders, and this is one of them. I know the issues, don't worry."

We resumed work. My heart wasn't really in it, I have to be honest, and I didn't think his was either. Could I trust him? Was this a ploy to bring me back to his side? All I knew was a state of utter confusion.

Grandad was late down for dinner. We heard him coughing quite severely, so much that I went to help him. Before we returned to the dining room, he spoke confidentially to me in between gasping a little for breath.

"She'll have rigged the witnesses. They'll swear that he's guilty and say they heard him denounce either Ahab or the Lord."

"Grandad, that will be untrue. That's awful."

He took a long moment. "It won't be the last time that trumped-up charges of blasphemy will send a good man to his death, Eran."

"Do you think he'll die, Grandad?"

He coughed uncomfortably before nodding, firstly to agree and secondly as if he needed a doze.

Ten minutes later, Sharon came back. Dad greeted her return with a loud sigh as she went straight to her room. I looked at Grandad. He was fast asleep in his chair. He hadn't touched a single morsel.

He stirred when she returned. I'd been worrying about him of late, so this was a relief. Sharon was apologetic. "Sorry, I was fixing my own make-up. The queen gave me some she didn't want. I'm back at the palace later."

My question and my manner were urgent. "Never mind that. What went on at the trial?"

"I wasn't there, Eran, but some of the staff were sent to support the prosecution case. They came back relieved."

"Oh good! So Naboth wasn't found guilty?"

She shook her head. "Oh, he was, of course. They weren't needed. The staff, I mean. They couldn't face doing what they were told. Naboth was an old friend of the older catering staff."

Dad agreed. "Oh, of course. They couldn't stand up to the court and defend Naboth. Not if they wanted to keep their jobs."

Mum wasn't impressed. "I'd say it was more about keeping a head on their shoulders. I get that."

Sharon was on the same page. "They were feeling bad about that. He was well liked, Naboth. A quiet, respectable supplier and a reliable, kind man of integrity."

Mum's tone was quiet but measured. "It's a pity they didn't proclaim his innocence, then. Shame on them."

Dad glared at her, then at me. For once, I agreed with him. "You wouldn't be saying that if your daughter was part of that group, Ayala. It's not that easy."

Mum pushed past him and left us to the food. No-one had had much of an appetite, it seemed. I was left with my thoughts. It was certainly hard to make a stand for the Lord when the chips were down. Much easier to run away. Wasn't that what Elijah had done? Had he backed down in the face of evil?

Shaz took me aside as she left to return to the palace. She looked around the street before whispering to me. "Two witnesses were taken from prison this morning. They are convicted criminals. The word is that a deal was done. Condemn Naboth and they'd go free."

"Oh, that's great. Not. So, they did?"

"With gusto. They went for it. Naboth didn't speak."

"So, what happened?"

"Much shrugging of shoulders, a short discussion, and a guilty verdict. That's all I know."

Dad's voice hit us full on. Whispering isn't for someone who is always right. I spun around and saw him in the doorway behind us. Sharon had missed him when she'd checked. He'd heard it all.

He wasted no time in joining the conversation. "I can tell you more, Sharon. They took him away to be stoned to death. It was over quickly."

I did the maths. Dad had left me in the fields around the time of the court sitting and returned a couple of hours later. How could he possibly know what had happened if he hadn't been at the stoning? Had he merely watched, or was he throwing the missiles that killed a good man? If so, no wonder he was speaking to me out of character. Had his demeanour been changed by the trauma of guilt? Certainly, seeing a human life taken isn't something you get over easily. Nagging at my mind was the thought that my father could be not just passive in Jezebel's terror campaign, and I hated myself for thinking it.

2 6

MOTHBALLS

The next day brought confirmation that the king had sequestered the vineyard. The word was that Jezebel had sent Ahab himself to claim the land as soon as she had proof of Naboth's death. Couldn't she just have sent a couple of palace guards? It was like she was asserting her power, not over the people, but over her husband. Ahab? He's done what he was told.

That evening, Sharon's return to the family was earlier than usual. It was just a break, apparently, but one during which she revealed a development which was remarkable, dangerous, and encouraging. Elijah had been granted an audience with Ahab. He was back in the vicinity of Jezreel.

"Him again? I'm astonished that our king gives him any time whatsoever. Surely, he's caused enough trouble! If it hadn't been for his magic tricks on Mount Carmel, we wouldn't be in this mess." I could have predicted Dad's words for him, if he hadn't been so reasonable with me in the fields. The swagger was back.

"Manny, this is nothing to do with Mount Carmel. This is

to do with yesterday's murder and theft." Mum had spotted his deflection tactic.

I waited till Grandad's cough had retreated. "Unless you know more than we do, Father." My questioning tone drew a dark paternal glance before Shaz spoke up.

"I know more about Elijah's visit, Dad. Obadiah smoothed the way diplomatically with Jezebel, by offering a route to stifle any budding revolt from the nation. He was clever, Obadiah. Jezebel allowed him to meet the king."

Was this further shift in power? It sounded that way. I made an observation. "What do you mean? Obadiah's never been a man to compromise on his beliefs."

Mum murmured her agreement as Shaz went on. "He was clever. He didn't. Let me tell you what happened in the meeting. Elijah spelt out the consequences of the regime's ongoing abuse of the Lord. He told him that peace would only come when the Lord was restored to His rightful place."

"Brave man." Dad's ironic tone was followed by a smirk.

Sharon shook her head. "Yes, Dad, he is. He told Ahab he had to repent and return to the God of Israel. Or else. He's got Ahab seriously worried."

Mum looked quizzical. "Or else?"

Sharon bit her lip and looked at us all before clarifying those two chilling words. "If he doesn't, then the Lord will visit His punishment upon them. Effectively, He will put a contract out on our king."

I was worried for Shaz. "I presume that includes Jezebel, Sis?"

I realised why she was less concerned. "Well, she doesn't

think so. She's furious with Elijah though. Obadiah's only safe because the eyes of the nation are on the palace."

"She won't have Elijah bumped off, then?"

Grandad's breathing was irregular as he heard that name. Did he shake his head? Probably. Mum's voice was full of reassurance. "I don't think so, no. I'm convinced that Elijah is under the close protection of the Lord. Just think back over the time since he first appeared on the scene. Elijah is the Lord's voice."

Shaz had more to tell, I thought. "Come on, Sis, if that's the case, surely Jezebel is in trouble too."

"That's the part she rejected when Ahab told her. He informed her that the death threat is on the king and the queen. She isn't going to get a royal send-off either, when it happens. Her beautiful body is going to be consumed by dogs."

Dad kept his counsel. My thoughts went to the immediate future. "Will it be the full sackcloth and ashes routine then?"

Shaz didn't know. "Maybe. I can't quite see those elegant royal robes going into mothballs, though."

Grandad tapped the table, but his head stayed low. A longer abrasive coughing fit shook the room. He settled again, in the same position. Sharon touched his arm and put her ear close to his face. "He's trying to speak. He's shaking. Help me! It's like he's going."

The old man wheezed four words to his beloved granddaughter, but they were meant for us all. "Believe in the Lord."

With that, his body fell limp as Sharon held him. She kissed him as Dad took Grandad from her. Dad included, we all wept bitterly.

27

EUPHORIA

The humble monarch routine surprised many. I guess it was about three months in total, with symbolic signs of royal regret from the king's side. Grandad's wisdom was sorely missed by yours truly, although there was the consolation of the inside track on events which Shaz was able to relate.

In short, she thought that there were two main schools of thought among the palace staff. The first was that Ahab was keen to preserve the advances he had made in developing the capacity of his military, so a superficial supernatural submission to his wife was a smart strategy. The second was that divine intervention bothered him significantly as it was the one force he knew he could not fight and defeat. Either way, no-one was buying the sincerity story. Too much had happened under the Ahab-Jezebel regime to convince anyone that the self-serving couple could countenance the supremacy of any other power than their own.

I worked hard to imagine what Grandad's view would have been. It struck me that firstly, the gods were being presented as a false, fake authentication of the king and queen's actions. Dear Grandad wouldn't have missed that. It must have happened many times in history, and no doubt would continue to happen in the future. To me, corruption and human leadership seemed rarely estranged bedfellows.

Shaz remained the queen's confidante throughout this time. However, she also spoke of a power battle which was being won exponentially by Jezebel. On more than one occasion, she commented how officials appeared to be reporting increasingly less to Ahab and proportionately more to his wife.

However, in the square, the word which eventually filtered down from Obadiah was that the Lord had stayed His hand over the threatened execution. Maybe there was some element of sincerity in Ahab's behaviour after all?

There was no point in seeking Dad's opinion. He would bluster his way through his usual pro-royalty speech, telling me I needed to give them elbowroom for wielding their rightful authority. It saddened me slightly that a person of his intelligence could disregard his powers of critical appraisal as he did. It wasn't always his way, I reminded myself, but really since around the time when Shaz had got her job at the palace. Was it misplaced loyalty? Possibly, but it felt like he was being controlled, in their power.

Mum, though, was measured. She observed that the Lord was demonstrably a living God, in the way that Baal wasn't. I know she'd had her doubts in the past, but those compromises were to keep the peace with my father. Now she had returned to the fold, taking solace from the fact that the Lord could show mercy and patience for the good of His people.

I'd got there before her, to the point where I told her boldly that I had heard that it was Elijah himself who had pronounced on this stay of execution. The Lord had been giving Ahab his final chance to get his act together, I said, and in my view, Elijah was correct. Mum? She just told me I was turning into Grandad.

Latterly, Shaz had been evidencing a change of mood from the royals which she described as moving towards a bizarre kind of euphoria. I asked the obvious question when Dad was out.

"Shaz, do they realise the precariousness of their situation? There's a death threat on them. There's nothing cheerful about that, unless I'm missing something."

"Yes. They heard that directly from Elijah. It couldn't have hit Ahab any more forcefully than it did, and the king is aware that what Elijah says comes true. But a few weeks going by has made a difference."

"You mean the threat seems less potent with each passing day?"

"It's not that simple, Eran. It's true to some extent, but we have to remember that Jezebel staked her reputation on Baal. She's a proud lady with a stubborn streak, and my reading of her is that this character trait will not allow Elijah to win this one, Lord or no Lord. She simply cannot countenance it."

"So, what is she doing?"

"She's working on the king's own pride. She told me she'd suggested that he should man up and not be cowed by some weirdo who has no military clout."

"Does he listen to her? And what about the rumours that she's adding constantly to her own powers? Is that true?"

"Eran, I'm only her make-up girl. It's woman-to-woman

chat, not political dogma we discuss. That said, my interpretation is that Ahab is weakening. Jezebel is undermining his repentant position, little by little. She's slowly moving him back towards trusting in Baal. That's my interpretation, Brother."

"I get that, Shaz. What about growing her own position?"

"She doesn't see it as that. She still tells me that she is having to add to her job description because the king is disinterested in all matters but the military. She says that the regime will fail if she doesn't step in."

"Is she being truthful, Shaz?"

"That's irrelevant, Eran. I think she believes it. It's like she's a reluctant heroine."

"In her opinion."

"Exactly. But remember his evil deeds still define him. Passing the responsibility on does not diminish his guilt."

I have to say that Elijah's words felt less powerful to everyone, royal or not, as time passed. Even in the square, there were a few doubters. The persecution of the Lord's followers had ended, leaving a feeling of nervy tolerance among the people. There was an insecurity in the air. The certainty with which the population had received Elijah's words had drifted into something characterised by lethargy. Mum was different. Her belief in the Lord grew stronger by the day. For her, the Lord was the one who held the reins.

I was chatting it all over with her one day, highlighting the latest thoughts of the cognoscenti in the square.

She stared me full in the face. "Eran, when those people in the square are doubting, will you give them something to think about?"

I smiled. "It depends on what you mean, Mother."

She was deadly serious. "I have a different perspective for them to consider. God's time is not the same as ours, Son. I believe the Lord is giving respite to all His people, not just the king and queen, because He loves everyone. The famine was terrible, and we are having a period of relative stability to restore us. Three years is nothing to a God who created the world in seven days, Eran."

"So, what's the word I give them, Mum?"

"Simple. God's punishment is coming if we do not return to Him and His ways, and that includes them as well as Ahab and Jezebel. All of us."

28

LIAISON

One hot and dry day sometime later, I was passing through the square when one of the regulars called me over. His words made me wonder if the end of the Lord's gracious delay was about to hit us.

"Eran, you'll know. Tell me, what's your definition of a warmonger?"

I wouldn't have known that, were it not for recalling a question I once asked of Grandad. I remember where I was when I asked him what one was, after Dad had been mouthing off.

Dad had gone out, I recall, before he told me. I used his words exactly as I remember them. "Warmonger? Usually, a senior military man who won't need to be in the front line of whatever he causes."

The reason why I had been stopped in the square, it turned out, was on account of rumours of a new conflict with Aram. This time they were not invading again, nor were their forces on our border.

It was the other way round. A disputed territory by the

name of Ramoth Gilead. It had been claimed and occupied by Aram. Our king wanted it back.

Sharon had an alternative view when we were at home that evening. "Yeah, Jezebel has been talking about that place for a while. She's convinced it belongs to our nation. Historically, she has proof, she tells me."

"So, the momentum towards conflict is coming from our own dear king. I thought that he was keeping under the radar."

"Jezebel's being very positive with him about the army he has built. She speaks to me of her pride in his military achievements."

"Is this really about the queen's power again, Shaz?" I was pretty sure of myself.

"She promotes herself as still covering the king's workload while he builds up his forces, if that's the same thing. She's been encouraging some diplomacy too, in the light of that. She's persuaded him to meet with King Jehoshaphat from the southern kingdom a couple of times recently, which he did. They're on good terms these days."

I had heard talk of this but was unsure of whether to be pleased or worried. "Jehoshaphat's a godly man, I believe. Everything he does, he prays to the Lord about."

I couldn't stop myself from wondering if Ahab would be strengthened somehow in his own faith. On the grand scale of things, this seemed a positive development. Our divided kingdom remains split between a divided people and has been for a long time. Sometimes it's been very bitter. The drive for a better relationship has got to be good, but how much of it is coming from Jehoshaphat? I suspected that this liaison was not on Jezebel's agenda for her husband.

I came back to the more pressing issue of a war. Would Ahab do as Jehoshaphat and consult our God on the matter? Or would he cave in to Jezebel and just take advice from his sycophantic officials?

The answer came from an unlikely source. Another prophet, Micahia, gained an audience with Ahab after Obadiah had accredited his authenticity with the king. The night beforehand, Micahia had not kept quiet about his intentions, these being that he would inform his Majesty that the Lord required him to consult all His prophets about his plans for military action and seizing of Ramoth Gilead.

Micahia was entertained by Ahab as agreed, but putting it simply, he was not seen ever again. Shaz had been in a session with Jezebel whilst the king's meeting was on. An official had knocked and entered, then had spoken to the queen. Sharon heard every word. Jezebel told Shaz to wait, leaving the room to, as it turned out, have a shouting match with Ahab. The prophet was taken out at the queen's command with a charge of treason on his head.

Three weeks later, the campaign to retake Ramoth Gilead came to a critical point. The battle ensued.

Soon after, the word went around the town that Ahab was expected shortly, returning in triumph. Protocol was that we all hit the streets.

It wasn't an option, to be honest, even for the queen. We were all there to cheer Ahab home. Dad's demeanour was irritatingly triumphal, beaming at me and Mum. Shaz was obviously at work. The queen had to look sensational. The king would return in his chariot, in his battle gear, the full armour, after reclaiming the land from Aram. Behind him would be Jehoshaphat. Both monarchs would be waving to the cheering crowd.

Dad's words were quite telling. "Our nation, the twelve tribes, will be reunited in glory." Such a victory parade, overseen by his heroine Jezebel, was to be everything his heart could have hoped for.

It was easy to forget that the Lord was still to play His hand. Ahab's days were numbered not that long ago. Micahia, it seems, had caused the shouting match by throwing his own ideas into the argument. Inflammatory didn't come into it. The doomed prophet told the pair of them that the kingdom of Ahab was rotten to the core. Sharon got that told to her loud and clear from the queen.

The rumour began to spread that there would be nothing to celebrate until the nation turned back to the Lord in repentance. It made sense. If we allow evil to guide us, or pray to another god, we are certain to deserve His punishment. We were, and are, called to be the chosen people of our God.

29

COMB

It got me questioning why we had a king in the first place. There had been one or two good ones, but a load of trouble too. It wasn't the ideal system. Grandad used to tell us that even the good ones got it wrong. Ahab wasn't high on his list, and in all truth, I knew his lady wife had been recruited by the devil many moons ago.

Uncertainty gripped the crowd, but no-one knew why. Dad found us, but of Shaz there was no sign. Families were expected to be together, united in their glorification of their king. I was anxious to find her. Mum was, as always, a voice of calm. "She's been attending to the queen. She must have over-run."

Then the chanting started. There was relief around us, but my thoughts were different, certainly to my father's. This was Ahab's glorious return, yet the celebrations were hollow.

The cry went up of a sighting of his chariot in the distance. He was on approach, just a few minutes away. However, as anticipation grew, Sharon found her way to us. Something was seriously wrong.

I spotted it first. "Hey, Shaz, what's happened to your face? You're bleeding!"

She began to sob. "It was Jezebel. She had a message to say matters had not turned out quite as expected. That's all I knew, so I asked her if she'd like me to pray for her, like Grandad used to say when things went wrong. But she went mad at me. Grabbed a comb and slashed at my cheek. I turned and ran. A friend of mine on the staff gave me a pad for the wound, but I just had to get out of there."

I thought I'd spotted the underlying issue. "Is this delivering another win for Elijah, Shaz? Is that why she's gone for you? Jezebel's prayers, such as they were, went to Baal. Total victory in battle would have justified her and those who follow her. Hearing that was not going to happen made her angry."

"Why me, though? In her head, I was as close to being her friend as anyone could get."

"It's human nature to strike out at your nearest and dearest, Shaz." Mum joined in, as soothingly as she could in the circumstances.

Dad saw things differently. "It's not a terminal condition, Sharon. Little more than a scratch. Listen, I hear the horses."

Horses there were, but no Ahab. Those who made it back into Jezreel did not have the air of conquerors. The only chariot in the sad procession was both plain and empty. The crowds began to drift away.

The king's whereabouts engaged those who remained. Speculation mounted that he may have been injured or taken prisoner. No-one mentioned the thought that he might even be dead, but in their heart of hearts, many present remembered the message of Elijah and the judgement of the Lord. Was this what had taken place? And where was Jehoshaphat?

It was Obadiah who took charge. He called the city elders together, who were to cascade the news throughout the city. Ahab was dead. The battle had been a disaster. Jehoshaphat and Ahab had been defeated. Obadiah confirmed that Yahweh had carried out His contract.

I looked at Dad. Oddly, he was smiling. Whimsically, maybe, but why?

Mum looked at him. "I wonder if this is the end of the road for the king's family too."

Sharon glanced nervously at Dad. "I'm staying off work for a while. I feel sick."

Dad's next remark threw me. Was he being serious? "Quite right, Sharon. I'm not letting any daughter of mine go anywhere near that palace. You're to stay at home."

Mum nodded. "And we'll get that slash to your face properly sorted."

I was emboldened. "I'm going to help Obadiah. I'll see you around. I'll get the full story about Ahab."

30

ARCHER

Obadiah didn't answer when I knocked at his house that evening. I was expecting that. He was keeping everything together at the palace and managing a tricky situation with Jezebel. His servant was with him. There was no-one at home.

The next morning, I was back. To my surprise, he invited me in. I began hesitantly. "Erm, it was me who…"

"You are Manny's boy. Brother of Sharon. I've been wanting to speak to you."

I couldn't believe it. "Thank you, Sir. My name is Eran." That was the best I could manage.

I needn't have worried. "I know your name, Eran. We met previously, if you remember."

Me remember? As if meeting a great man happened to me every day. But that couldn't be why he had a message for me.

He smiled. "You probably don't know that yesterday's events were not unexpected. The truth is that the situation in the palace has been deteriorating over many months, but more intensively over the last few weeks. The death of the king in battle was a certainty, to me. The Lord's purposes cannot be thwarted by mere mortals."

"How did it happen, Sir?"

"Eran, reports speak of a division of enemy soldiers spotting a chariot. They gave chase and forced it into a corner."

"So, Ahab died like that?"

"Oh no, it wasn't him. They'd found Jehoshaphat. The southern kingdom monarch, not the one they were looking for."

"So, they killed him anyway?"

"No, they left him sitting there, rather bemused."

"Why? Wouldn't his head have been a trophy for them back in Aram?"

"Eran, I'm told you will understand this. Can you see the hand of Yahweh? Jehoshaphat is faithful to Him. This was no ordinary battle."

I could. "So, Jehoshaphat was spared because of his faith?"

"Exactly. But not Ahab. They went off to locate his chariot. The task was made harder by the fact that he was wearing civvies over his armour, not the robes of his office."

I was respectful. "Sir, That must have been a battle tactic. I suppose Ahab did die for his faith. It was just the wrong one."

He stroked his chin. "Look, Eran, we are commanded to love the one true God. The Lord had given him time to bring our nation back to Himself, and then extra time too. He couldn't do it. There's a warning to us all there."

I knew I'd need more detail for the family. "Sir, under his disguise, Ahab had metal plates and bands covering every weak point of his body. He was practically invincible. Isn't that right?"

Obadiah smiled. "Man's attempts to thwart our God are a mere distraction."

"So how did he die? What saw the king off?"

"An archer fired an arrow. It found a chink in his armour."

I let out a low whistle. "That arrow had to be guided by the Lord. If not, it had to be a shot in a million. Did he die there, on the spot? Or did he carry on fighting, encouraging his men by example?"

"Not at all, Eran. He did what you might expect. He told his entourage to get him out of there. They made him as comfortable as they could, then did as he told them. His blood couldn't be stopped. It stained the chariot floor. He died because of his wounds."

"So where is his body?"

"In the city of Samaria. He's already buried there. It is the place Ahab's father Omri built."

"And the chariot?"

"Good question. They're saying they cleared the blood pools from the floor crevices using dogs to lick it out. There wasn't much respect in that. He was a king, however bad. Do you recall the dreadful Naboth outrage? Blood licking was what Yahweh told him would occur. We should not be surprised. When they washed the chariot, the water they used came from where the local ladies of the night have a wash."

"Really, Sir?"

"Eran, our God's punishment is as powerful as it is inevitable for those who reject Him."

"I understand. What happens to the queen? She lashed out at Sharon yesterday, as you may know."

"I'm sorry to hear that, Eran. I'm not surprised. The queen

hasn't had a civil word for anyone of late, blaming all but herself."

"Sir, isn't she under the same sentence as her late husband?"

"She is, Eran. It's only a matter of time. How she'll cope with the next king, I don't know. That's their son, of course, Ahaziah. He'll be based in Samaria, by all accounts. Not here."

"Will that improve anything?"

"With Ahaziah? There might be a bit of peace where we live if he's not around. However, even that's questionable. People's greater fear is that he'll be even worse than Ahab."

"More misery, then?"

"Eran, it will be temporary, if anything. Ahab was clearly told that the wrath would fall on his family too, and Ahaziah is very much under that prophecy."

I apologised for undue impatience in what I was about to say. "The problem I find with Yahweh is that sometimes I just wish He would crack on with it. A good lightning strike with accompanying thunderbolt and they're wiped out."

Obadiah acknowledged me with a hint of a smile. "I know. We all think we know how the Lord should do His stuff. But hey, He's not just dealing with our problems, is He? He's got a whole world of issues to sort out. Listen, Eran, you go home now. Look after your sister. She's a good girl. She might be out of a job if Jezebel goes with our incoming monarch and settles in Samaria."

3 1

GONER

Well, Jezebel did just that. One day, she was gone. There was some sense of relief around Jezreel, but the unseen grip of underlying evil was still holding sway. A puppet official ensured the new regime's orders were announced and implemented in our city. It felt to me that my father was a lonely voice at times, proclaiming the virtues of the new king and justifying his mother's outrageous behaviour. Never mind their Jezreel spokesperson's strings, Ahaziah's were being pulled by she who was to be obeyed.

Sharon, it seems, was irreplaceable to Jezebel. Was it fear which drove her to accept Jezebel's contract, or was there more to it? Shaz played the grandad card in their discussions, and Jezebel gave Sharon somewhere pretty smart to live, with permission for occasional return visits to us in Jezreel, to be taken at her discretion. Jezebel's discretion, that was.

It was many months later when Shaz got back. Even after so long, her leave of absence had been in jeopardy at the last minute after the fallout from a royal incident, but once the queen's eye was off the ball, Shaz left as planned.

"What happened, Shaz?" I had to know.

"Just before I left, Eran, she'd given Ahaziah a blast in his ear. She was furious with him. It seems he'd found the last case of Naboth's last vintage which they took when they moved, got a couple of his mates round and got absolutely bladdered."

"Ahaziah got drunk? But she drinks as much as he does, doesn't she?"

"More, if her hangovers are anything to go by. Our morning conversations are defined by no more than the odd grunt, and never anything controversial."

"So, there was more to it than an overdose of the jolly juice, Shaz. Why would she be angry if she's as guilty as he is? What's happened?"

"Okay, so it appears that he's staggered towards his bed, missed his grab at the handle and gone through the ventilation panel. He's in a mess. Multiple fractures. Cuts, bruises. Some of them have turned nasty."

"Didn't his drinking mates hear the crash?"

"They must have done, but they would have been far gone too. They probably just laughed. It seems that no-one thought it was serious. So, no-one went up to have a look."

"So, the queen found him lying there in a drunken stupor, right?"

"You've got it in one. It didn't stop her berating the man. She told me she slammed the door on him and returned to her room."

"Didn't she realise his condition? Or at least get help? He's her son, after all."

"Drinking to excess is a terrible distorter of reasoning.

Jezebel saw fit to let him stew in his own juice. It was left to me to deal with matters this morning."

"I don't get you. Get the king on the mend through the doctors and you're back doing her wardrobe and make-up, right. And she runs the show as usual."

"Not exactly. That blazing row in the night left the other staff too scared to go, so I had to take charge and summon the doctors. There was no sign of the queen at this point."

"Sorry, Shaz. You were brave."

"Well, I was the only option. My relationship with her was the best among the staff, so even if she'd disliked my decision, she probably wouldn't have punished me harshly."

"So, what did the doctors say?"

"That there was nothing they could do. They broke the news in stages. I stayed in the room, then Jezebel came in. She was there for the first instalment. Ahaziah came over all spiritual after they told him he wouldn't walk again."

"Don't tell me he was tempted to turn back to the Lord".

"Eran, I thought the same thing. But after the doctors had told him to prepare for end-of-life care, Jezebel came up with an alternative. It appears that there's another option for getting cured. It's a god who they claim can see into the future. He hangs out spiritually in a temple at Ekron."

"Right, and he predicts the future, you say. A kind of prophet?"

"In a dodgy kind of way, Eran. Personally, I don't see how a god can be his own prophet, but there you go. Baal-Zeebub is the name. Ahaziah has already sent his messengers there."

"To see what lies ahead for him? I wonder what the devil

Baal-Zeebub will come up with?" Rampant cynicism oozed through my tone and made Sharon smile.

"Not a lot. The king has no future. But that's not all. One of my colleagues updated me further as I was leaving. The queen is absolutely belligerent, and that's putting it mildly."

"Surely what she thinks doesn't matter, Shaz. The Lord's hand is on this."

"It would seem so, Eran. My friend also had heard that Elijah has been commissioned by an angel to go and head off these emissaries at the pass."

My spirits lifted. "Praise the Lord! He's moving in all this. So, this double-barrelled deity won't get the pleasure of prophesying anything!"

"Eran, the Lord is returning these messengers to the palace in Samaria. Elijah is accompanying them, and his job is to tell Ahaziah that he is a total goner."

I shouldn't have asked this, but it slipped out anyway. "Won't that put Elijah's own future in jeopardy?"

Shaz put me to shame. "No, don't forget that Elijah trusts in the Lord, who won't leave him undefended. We should be doing that too."

"True. Dear Elijah has a track record of doing most of what our God asks of him. How's he going to feel about this one?"

"Well, I was told that Obadiah is backing Elijah to do the job. This is too important. Obadiah thinks the Lord will embolden Elijah and the full force of the message will reach the stricken king."

I inhaled sharply. "Sounds like he's going to be more than stricken shortly."

Sharon nodded. "I'm only home for a couple of days. The queen will need me. The rest of my leave can wait."

Her words confused me. She was praising God and encouraging me to be stronger, yet here she was, forty-eight hours into her first holiday for a couple of years and she's going back into the teeth of the gale. "You don't feel loyalty to her, do you?"

"Loyalty? No. I have a job to do. Familiarity breeds understanding. I get what's below the surface with her. Think of me as moderating her outbursts wherever I can."

It still didn't add up. I made a decision. Dad wouldn't do this, but I would. "Shaz, I'm worried. Never mind the farm, I'm coming to Samaria with you."

3 2

MARBLES

I've never considered myself a leader in the world of fashion but despite the features God had given my face, I could scrub up when necessary. However, the ragged state of dress I was in after that long trek to Samaria with Sharon left me dumbfounded.

Not her. "Look any scruffier and they'll mistake you for Elijah!"

The great man was certainly not into power dressing, a concept of which he had no need. His power was directly from the Lord rather than from his dress sense, I thought, and as I reflected on his lifestyle, it made sense. His call to all our nation and to anyone else who cares to listen was to repent and turn back to our God. Obadiah was right, Elijah humbles himself because the Lord is greater.

In Samaria, stories abounded of how the king's men were intercepted and their destination revised. The twin-surnamed deity was denied. Obadiah courageously reminded his listeners that all this was fulfilling the Lord's earlier judgement on Ahab's family.

The rumours went that the three of them turned round and trotted off to tell Ahaziah that he'd had it. However it happened, the king was lying there, expecting some good news, of course. His mum was in the room too.

The queen is alleged to have laughed. Ahaziah didn't even crack a smile, so the queen told him to send soldiers to fetch Elijah to him. He did so. An army captain with fifty of his men. But the arrest did not pass off without trouble. The captain made a mistake. He called Elijah 'Man of God'. Given the state of Elijah's attire, I guess he might have been using irony. With fifty armed men on his side, was an error possible? Indeed, it was. They became no use to him very quickly. Putting it simply, our God barbecued them.

How? Let me tell you. Elijah asked the Lord to prove to the captain that he, Elijah, really was a man of God. So, the Lord created a fireball and wiped these unbelievers out. When the king heard of this, the king's mum made him send another captain and fifty.

You are probably guessing what happened, and you are probably not wrong. Same story, same words, same fate. But there was a twist in the tale.

She despatched a third captain with…yes, fifty armed soldiers. But no fire this time. He brought his men safely back to the palace. This captain was wise. He didn't refuse the mission, though, they went there alright. But the officer humbled himself in front of Elijah. Can you imagine the sight? A military man, armed, in a splendid uniform, prostrating himself before this scruffy old hobo lookalike?

He was sincere. He pleaded for his life. This one meant it when he called him 'Man of God'. The third fireball was called off. Then Elijah suggested that they all went back to the palace together. Had he lost his marbles? Was he mentally a few sandwiches short of a picnic?

Obadiah always maintains that Elijah has been given some of the hardest tasks any human has ever been asked to complete. This was right up there. He went to see the king. The queen was also there. Ahaziah heard the death sentence straight from the sartorially challenged prophet's mouth. A moment later, he was dead. He died in front of them as soon as the message was delivered.

Jezebel? She screamed blue murder. I was glad Shaz didn't have to deal with her when that happened. As you will recall, Jezza, as we used to call her once upon a time, is down for the same fate as her husband and her son. All she could do was to watch and wait for wipeout.

Joram, the queen's younger son, was next in line for the throne. Samarian folks suggested he wasn't great either, but he turned out to be somewhat irrelevant to our tale. All eyes were on the queen.

Routine eventually made a semblance of a return as things settled down. Reassured, I decided I could undertake the long journey home. It was almost four months later when Shaz arrived back, full of excitement at the latest sensation.

33

CLOAK

"Eran, he's gone! Chariot job. We just got word from Obadiah. You are the first in Jezreel to hear it."

I was on the ball immediately. "Are you talking Elijah here? And if so, where?"

She nodded. "So, you know who Elisha is, right?"

I did. "He's the dude lined up to take over from the main man, yeah? He's been on apprenticeship since they met."

"Yes, that's him, Eran. So, him and Elijah, right, they'd not long been on the road from Gilgal."

Geography wasn't my strongest suit. "Jericho area, Gilgal?"

"That's the one. There, they nearly split up."

"You mean the partnership was almost over? The apprenticeship was finished? Surely not!"

"Steady, Eran. Elijah told Elisha to stay put while he went off to Bethel."

I wondered if Elisha had been over-doing things and needed a break. Shaz went on. Apparently, this was not the case. He wasn't up for the split, so they went to Bethel together. There, the prophets – God's people like me – came out to meet them, but they took Elisha to one side. They told Elisha that the Lord was taking his boss from him the same day. To heaven.

You might think of the parallel of the Samarian palace scenes. How did Elisha react? Was it a great shock to the apprentice? Not the case either. Elisha told them that he knew already, and that was his reason for not leaving Elijah's side.

The departure point wasn't Bethel, though. There was a repeat of the same thing, this time in Jericho. Elijah told them that the Lord was guiding him to where he was going. It certainly keeps everyone fit, all this walking. And when he got there? Elisha was taken to one side and again told that the Lord would be taking Elijah to heaven that day. Elisha instructed them to keep it quiet. Not a dicky bird to anyone on the subject.

You won't be surprised to know that there was a third episode which started the same way. Elijah says he'll go on alone to where waters flow. The Jordan. Elisha decides he won't let him out of his sight, and fifty of the prophets, the Lord's people, decide to do the same thing. They follow behind.

My mind strayed immediately back to the mountain top and the fire scenarios. You will recall that those events also involved fifty soldiers at a time. Don't worry, Elisha's lot didn't get incinerated, but an amazing thing took place. Elijah took off his cloak. To the world, it wasn't exactly resaleable, for reasons of inadequate quality. To the watching world, his was not a king among cloaks, but Elijah rolled it up tightly and dealt a hefty blow with the resulting bundle to the surface of the water. This garment was a symbol of his role as a spokesman for the Lord. It was beyond price.

Was he frustrated with Elisha not leaving him in peace and now bringing fifty spectators to ensure he was okay? Over fussy, maybe? I didn't know. But then, it seems, the water parted. Elijah and Elisha walked across the dry bed of the Jordan.

Of course, that rang a bell from the past. The resonance with history was clear, but there was a difference. The army of prophets weren't drowned. They didn't do any pursuing. Then they spoke briefly. Elijah knew what was about to happen, he had known all along. He asked Elisha what his last wish would be.

That was the wrong way round, wasn't it? I was sure that the one who was about to die usually got the last wish.

How stupid I felt! He wasn't about to die. Anyway, Elisha asked to inherit the spirit of Elijah, only twice as strongly.

In material terms, I don't suppose the former ever fancied the cloak, but it was so much more than that. Taking it would symbolise the Lord's blessing on our young prophet as Elijah's true successor, but it was a tough ask. Just think what Elijah had been through. Could he wish that on his young friend? Tricky. He just told him that if he could see him after he had gone, the wish would be granted. If not, then he would be disappointed.

Your big question is…did he see him afterwards? Well, they started walking alongside the river. They were split up. Me, I thought Elijah had got his wish, hey? A break from Elisha! But this was permanent. It was by chariot. And here's the fire. The chariot and the horses appeared to be made of it.

They took him away, a twisting wind, so strong, it lifted him away and up to the skies. He'd gone in the hot seat. Wow!

3 4

GUARANTORS

So, did Elisha see him after he'd been whisked away? He did, he saw it all. The Lord be praised! Elisha was the new Elijah. The apprentice had become the master. And there's going to be more mighty deeds as our God works out His purposes through Elisha.

What happened to that old cloak? Elisha saw it and picked it up with commendable environmental awareness, but actually, he knew fully what he was accepting. He struck the river in the way Elijah had done. The river parted and he walked back. The Lord held the river back for him. Momentous. He was shaking afterwards.

You would, wouldn't you? Major miracle, first solo show. It makes me tremble at the thought.

Did the prophets just walk home after a day to remember? No, not the case. The prophets saw and prostrated themselves before Elisha. Then they decided they ought to carry out a search for Elijah.

Three whole days they dedicated to the hunt. No sign of the chap, no chariot tracks nor scorch marks. Having done that, they stood as witnesses and guarantors of the truth of what happened.

I couldn't help but wonder what Jezebel would be making of all this. To me, her world of idolatry was collapsing in front of her.

I had to wait many months for Shaz to complete a final stint at the Samaria palace before she returned to Jezreel for the last time.

"What's the story, Shaz? It's all over, I guess."

"When I got back, Eran, I began to see that the pagan believers have taken a severe battering. Even in the palace, the whispers were that the Lord was at work through Elisha, although Jezebel didn't see things that way. She was fighting. Then there was this thing about the water. We all know how the Lord made the rain fall to prove he was the only God in existence, and that all the other so-called deities were no more than lumps of wood and metal? Remember that amazing moment with Elijah on Mount Carmel!"

"Oh yes, Elijah was watching from a cave, as I recall. What a great way to bring an end to the famine too! Who could ever forget the immense feeling of relief back then? Nice one God!"

"Well, it wasn't quite that simple. It seems there was an ongoing problem with the water supply in Jericho. It had become tainted. It was horrible to drink and no good for the farmers either. It caused a bit of a stink."

"So, do tell what happened to the smell from hell?" I grinned.

"Elisha got them to fetch a bowl of salt. Then he threw it in, at the source of their spring. And it cured the problem immediately. They were blown away. But that wasn't all. There was the abuse of the hairline."

I didn't get it. "What?"

"Well, Elisha has been, how shall we say, personally challenged, over having no hairstyle for a number of years. That's because he's got nothing to style. Some yobbish youths came out and kicked off on him. They called him 'baldy', which he did not need to be reminded of."

I had to ask. "Do we know if he had problems at the barber's as a younger man, Shaz?"

"Hmm. I gather he paid a search fee rather than a standard cut charge, if that helps. But like Elijah, he never considered himself a cut above the rest of society."

I smirked. "That's enough hair puns. Did he find parting was difficult?"

Shaz smirked back. "Moving on. What mattered was that the Lord needed His man to be seen to have His backing, hair or no hair."

"Good. What actually happened?"

"Two bears, that's what happened. They came out from the trees and set about the yobs. A few of them legged it back to the city, but forty-two of them received a good mauling for their troubles. They won't be doing it again."

I couldn't help but feel a sense of justice done. "Who sent these young hooligans? They don't usually move around in those numbers."

"Rumours in the palace were that it was a group organised by the queen. She's still resisting the Lord, incredibly. She's having to be careful. The new king is very much anti-Baal. Not that it has stopped him behaving as he chooses. He's as bad as the rest of them. Idol worship is still encouraged."

"Right. It's a credibility thing, I guess. Baal's public profile is not strong after Elijah's work, and Elisha is from the same mould."

Shaz paused. "Erm, yes, that's it. But the queen is holding firm. She is like a dog with a bone over Baal. She will not let it go. She's still fighting. My problem is that she has to look good for every potential influencer, and I'm still doing the make-up. She's not as young as she was. I now have to dress royal mutton as lamb."

"I prefer the canine image. Baal the bone idol. Seriously, though, it'll be the end of Jezebel. Where's Elisha now, Shaz?"

"He's safe in Samaria. No-one's going to argue with him there for a while, after the grizzly fate of those youths. Word spreads fast. He'll be fine. Her mind is on the troubles surrounding the Moab rebellion. She can't deal with it, but neither can she leave it alone."

That was almost the last I saw of Sharon. She just made her farewells and was gone, no major concerns about her journey back to Samaria or the life awaiting her. She was oblivious to the danger I knew so well. With my father firmly entrapped by his loyalty to Jezebel, I had my responsibilities to the family. An hour later, I gave chase.

I didn't have to chase too far. The city square, to be precise. No-one was there, strangely, but I heard a muttering from the hidden corner, and a scuffle of feet. A second later, Sharon emerged looking slightly dishevelled. As I moved towards her, did I see the figure of Joel disappearing in the distance? This was my moment. I would tell her everything. All Joel's treachery was about to be revealed.

"Eran, go home!"

"But Shaz…"

"Eran, I'm going back where I belong. With the queen. I have a job to do."

"You're in grave danger, Shaz. You don't know what you are going back to. I need to protect you. I'm coming with you."

"I don't need you, Eran. I have all the protection I need."

I gestured down the street to where I'd seen Joel. "Him? He's in league with the evil woman you serve. Trust him and you're dead."

She smiled. "I don't need you, Eran, nor your fancy theories. Now go home and dream up a few more spy games."

Gobsmacked didn't cut it. I was literally stunned. My mouth wouldn't move. Nor my arms and legs. She gestured at me, turned on her heel and went off. Towards the horizon recently vacated by Joel.

3 5

NARKED

"And that's as much as I know, Yesh." The present had returned, but he saw that I had not been able to leave the past in peace.

Yesh put his hand on my arm. "That's some story, Eran. But why did you come to live out here after that confrontation?"

I yawned, relaxing from my lengthy narrative. "She was foolish. I found this house, not too near or far from the palace, to wait for her when she realised. It would only be a matter of time, I thought. Family honour is important, Yesh."

"How do you mean, Eran?"

"I knew I wasn't the marrying kind, my friend. None of the girls ever gave me a second look. But I wanted to see the next generation and to give them a proper full childhood and adolescence, like I tasted as a kid but never got as I hit my teens. Sharon finding a decent bloke was my only hope."

"And you haven't tried to make any kind of contact with her in all the time you've been here." Was that a question or a statement? I didn't know.

"What, blow my cover? That'd be great, Yesh. Any more brilliant ideas?"

He nudged me gently. "You are still angry with her, aren't you? For treating you the way she did. And you're furious with your father and irritated by your mother. Am I reading you right?"

"I suppose so." Reluctance was all over my face.

Yesh took a deep breath. "Brace yourself."

I sat up straight and looked at him. His eyes were closed and he was praying. Moments later he began.

"When I arrived, I mentioned that I had something to tell you from your parents. Obadiah was with your dad when he died. In his last few moments, he gave him a message for you. That was passed to me, Eran. On his deathbed, your dad asked Obadiah to find you and tell you that he had always loved you and he hoped that one day, you would understand."

"Well, he had a funny way of going about it, Yesh. I suppose my mum had a word for me too."

"Not to Obadiah, but people claimed that, in later days, she often spoke of regret over your upbringing. She missed you, Eran. She wanted to make things right with you, but you'd gone."

I didn't respond to that one because my heart was burning.

"Eran, shall I complete your story for you?"

Internally, I was fighting disbelief mixed with a gamut of emotions. Part of me wanted to cry. I presumed he would tell me that Sharon had been a saint too. I was also still slightly narked, so I shook my head. "We've talked enough for one day. Tomorrow will be fine." And with that, I gritted my teeth, gave him the rest of the food I had, a bottle of my wine, and stomped off to bed. Hunger wouldn't hurt me. I'd been hungry before.

Next day, we were up with the sun. The irritations of the night before had dissipated with the morning mists.

"Eran, my escort will be here in an hour or so. The camel has to be back for a deadline, so let's talk. Let me tell you about the lady you call our dear queen."

He was avoiding family issues, I thought. Fine by me. "What evil is Jezebel perpetrating now, Yesh? Isn't she getting too old for this kind of behaviour?"

"None and no, my friend."

"This is what you promised to tell me before. She has passed away, Yesh, hasn't she? There's a family tree full of wickedness in her lot, so even if she's met a quiet end, the family trait will go on."

"Passed away? That doesn't do it justice. Let me tell you what took place, Eran. When the end came, there was drama, not that we were really expecting anything less. The Lord's hand was evident. Judgement was finally enforced. You don't mess with the God of Israel."

"Where did it happen, Yesh? In Samaria?"

"No! Back in Jezreel. I won't go into the details, but Joram was recuperating there after a battlefield wound. King Ahaziah, Jehoram's son, decided to pay him a courtesy visit. Unbeknown to this pair of monarchs, the Lord had instructed Elisha to anoint Jehu as king over both our kingdoms, while they were still reigning. Jehu, you may recall, was from the southern kingdom, the son of the previous, and now of course late, king, Jehoshaphat."

"That's right. So how did it all play out, Yesh?"

"Well, Eran, the King of Israel and the King of Judah decided to present a united front, fighting against the Lord's purposes. And more than that, it all ended on the site of Naboth's vineyard."

"So how did it all get resolved?"

"Well, to cut a long story very short, Jehu and his men used subterfuge to get the two of them together. Joram and Ahaziah were then told by Jehu that there could be no peace when idolatry flourished in the land. In short, they were in big trouble. He shot Joram with a single arrow and mortally injured him. Did Ahaziah stand his ground and fight? No, but they pursued and wounded him, and he died shortly after, in a place called Megiddo.

Jezebel? Remember it was she who originally wanted to possess that vineyard. She did what she was best at and tried to seduce Jehu. However, with no Sharon there to help, it was not a pretty sight. Her feminine charms were a bit wrinkly and shapeless without your sister's skills, and some supporting kit, to prop them up. She didn't get him as far as the bedroom door. She called to him from her window. She taunted him whilst beckoning him to come up."

"Did it work, Yesh?"

"No, he invited her to join him. The quick way, by which I mean defenestration. Out of the said window, high up. Jehu ordered some of her servants to supply the requisite push. Did they obey Jehu? They did. They'd had enough of her. She plunged to her death.

Royalty deserves respect, even in death. So, he saw that she got a proper burial, once his horses had wiped their feet on her. There was blood everywhere. Remember I told you she was once like a dog with a bone, wasn't she? Well, she became the bone. The dogs got to her. Skull, feet and hands was all there was left. Jehu ordered a slap-up dinner from the kitchen and enjoyed it whilst this was going on.

When he'd finished his dessert, he viewed the leftovers. Not from his meal, you understand. And he ordered the skull, feet and hands to be buried where she fell. In what was Naboth's vineyard. The irony did not escape Jehu. His unshakeable view was that he was carrying out the work of the Lord.

That was not the end. Jehu moved onto the case of all remaining relatives. The House of Ahab was wiped off the face of the earth. Totally eradicated. The family line came to a squalid end."

It took me more than a moment to comprehend the meaning of his words. The scenes he had just described were horrific, yet a voice in my head told me I would have no nightmares over them, and that my recurring dream involving Jezebel and that glinting blade would bother me no longer.

36

STRINGS

I took a deep breath. "Wow, Yesh. The House of Ahab taken out. All of them! It's hard to imagine the country free of all their cruelty." I managed to raise a grin.

Yesh returned the smile. "The Lord always honours His promises and does what is just. Justice demands more than we sometimes like to pretend."

One of my big questions came back into my head, one I had never resolved to my own satisfaction. "Why didn't He do it sooner, Yesh? It was pure evil, yet He let it run and run. It happened to His own people."

"Eran, we only see life from our own viewpoint. Obadiah once told me that the Lord has perfection in His timing. We need to wait on Him. We should not expect Him to fit in with our perceptions. We can be rather impatient, you know, even as His people."

"Obadiah means that we like to have God act as we would like Him to, right?"

"That's it, Eran, yes. But as a nation, we have moved far from Him. What right have we to treat Him, the Creator God, like some puppet whose movements we orchestrate? It's ludicrous."

"Some people are so shortsighted, Yesh. Unbelievably so."

"Right, Eran. Now, before my escort calls to take me home, I need you to summarise how you remember those closest to you."

He hadn't forgotten to talk family. I jumped straight in with the bare essentials. "Grandad was the best, as I said. Mum? She had a difficult task because of my father. Dad? He was a toe rag, a dog. He fell for Jezebel's tricks. He was seduced by her ideas if nothing else. He believed the bull. If Grandad was unsighted by torture, my father was blinded by a powerful woman who used her physical attributes to maximum effect. My father shared her hatred for Elijah and ridiculed Obadiah. Then there's Sharon. She betrayed me. She rejected my protection. She became a lacky to Jezebel under the guise of a make-up artist. I'd loved that girl as I should have done, and she threw it back in my face and went off with Joel."

"The young musician?" Joel was a common name.

"Him. He was shifty. Great to start with, a fan of Obadiah, supported Elijah, made all the right moves. He would have made a great brother-in-law. But he was sucked into the palace as the sands of time moved on, and then became like my father, I guess, pro Jezebel, serving her, reneging on all his beliefs. I lost all respect for the guy."

"And yourself, Eran?"

"I did what I had to do. I admit to a few wobbly moments over the Baal issues, but I matured into a firm follower of the Lord. I became a man of principle. Yesh, I am a faithful."

Yesh looked out and saw an approaching figure. "Nearly time I was off."

"The camel can't be late on my account. Go, Yesh. It's been good."

"May I bring my escort in for a moment, Eran?"

"If you've time, yes."

"You must promise to listen, Eran. I've heard what you had to say. Can you promise that?"

"Yes."

"Sure? No interruptions? Sure?"

This was getting irritating. As if I couldn't control my mouth. "Let's get on with it, Yesh. You're the one in a hurry."

He looked at me one final time. I thought he was going to ask me again. Who was this escort anyway? A Jezreel camel owner? What could he have to say that would change anything?

Yesh opened the door and brought in the hooded figure. The hood greeted me in a voice I knew. He pulled back the cloth covering to reveal his face. It was Joel, the traitor.

I was bursting to tell him what I thought of him. Treachery was the word on my lips as I stood. Yesh came between us with a finger on his lips and motioned me to sit down. I did as he indicated.

He spoke. "It wasn't all one way, Eran. Not all the people accepted Baal and his like."

I knew that. "Elijah hid around a hundred of them, didn't he?"

"He did. He did more than that too. But what do you think they did whilst they were in hiding?"

"Prayed, I guess. Maybe sang a few worship songs. But kept out of sight."

"That's what many people thought, Eran. But there's another story line here you don't know. Joel, will you tell Eran what you recounted to the city leaders in Jezreel recently?"

Joel took a deep breath and began. "Eran, hear me out. I know you hate me."

Not another trick or trap, I thought. If I was to believe him, all my questions would need answering, all the issues dealing with, all mysteries explained. I shook my head at him fiercely, but he went on.

"We'll start with Obadiah. He was quite a man. He foresaw the chaos and evil of the regime months before Jezebel and her hubby made their first move. So, he began to build a resistance. He arranged that Yesh's father, who was a faithful, was selected and inducted into the palace guard. To the outside world, it was a uniformed position of responsibility. To those who knew, he became the link between himself and the believers in the city square, whom he had always joined during his time off. No suspicions aroused, business as usual, but a channel established."

Fair enough, I thought, I could see Obadiah doing that. Yesh's dad was a regular bloke. I wanted to hear more.

"Next was a non-uniformed appointment to the network. Male, smart, with an ability to act."

My mum would have suggested that the first two criteria rendered the task impossible. Why for heaven's sake would a drama qualification be required? Joel pre-empted the question which I could not have asked anyway.

"Secretive, subtle. No tracks to be followed, no trails left.

An established function within the palace, a known role outside. Effectively, a man who could live a double life. Obadiah identified his chosen candidate, persuaded the king that he needed a head of security, convinced Jezebel that a mature but fit man was needed, and the job was his."

I rebuked myself as I realised that I was warming to Joel. Spies, clandestine deeds? This was my thing. At that moment, I couldn't see how it would help, hindsight revealing what it had done, but the latent secret agent in me was curious. I quite liked the sound of this chap. Was that it for Obadiah's resistance committee?

It wasn't. "Things happened at pace. Obadiah wanted female support too, to work under the man's guidance. He influenced the recruitment process to see a new, low-profile addition to what he called Jezebel's circus. Another player was in place."

Sharon must have known her, I thought. She'd talked of the other girls, but not by name. Maybe that was deliberate. I'd never be able to ask my sister, of course. As far as I was concerned, she had cut her ties with me, and I was not going to go crawling back.

Yesh spotted the fading smile in my eyes as it turned back to a glare of stubborn determination. He held up a hand to Joel.

"Eran, can we deal with your enmity towards Joel before we leave?"

I gulped. It was deep-rooted, not superficial. Yesh went on.

"He also was part of Obadiah's set-up. You haven't heard the full story. Joel knows more. We are running late as it is. Our time here is almost up. Why don't you come back with us to Jezreel, my friend? Can you set aside your anger for that time? Travel with us, at least as a companion. I can only promise you that it will answer your questions. Trust me."

Talk about short notice! Could I? Could I really? A small voice in my head was telling me I could. Joel smiled at me in a way he did when we first met. My curiosity had been aroused about Obadiah. I knew I couldn't have agreed to it yesterday, but something had changed today. All things are relative, remember, but I went to pack what I deemed to be the best of what I possessed. I then dressed in garments which were more appropriate to a rather dusty trip.

3 7

HYPOCRITES

It wasn't the easiest journey at my stage of life, but we camel-shared and did it in three days. Conversation was curtailed by restrictions of non-controversiality, but as we approached Jezreel, there seemed to be some kind of community festivity going on. The streets were decorated as they were when a battle had been won.

It was a strange feeling. Yesh insisted on lunch at an inn on the edge of the city whilst Joel returned the camel to its base. Food and water were welcome.

Yesh wiped his mouth with his serviette. "Well done, Eran. Time to join the celebrations. You need to attend the final event tonight."

I wasn't for attending anything. I'd been hooked by the promise of some truth and was expecting explanations. My heart wanted a few more spy revelations, if I'm honest, but would I get any? I wasn't sure. I explained my position to Yesh.

"No question. You have to be there. You'll regret it for the rest of your days if you don't attend. We are honouring

Obadiah at a public ceremony in the city square. You will stay here at my expense tonight. I will call for you when it's time to enter the city. Smart is the dress code, by the way, for tonight."

"Well, I'll do what I can with what I've got, Yesh."

"You've never been what I'd call a snappy dresser, mate, but I'm sure it'll do fine. People will just be overjoyed to see you."

As he spoke, Joel reappeared and gave Yesh a thumbs-up from a short distance away. The latter grinned. "I'm off to tell your story to the organisers and chroniclers. I'll leave Joel with you. You can mend a few bridges if you like, he's a faithful."

Faithful? Joel? That was challenging, given what I knew.

He started the bidding. "Eran, my wife would like to join us at some point this evening. We're asking a neighbour to look after the kids. Would you mind?"

I couldn't, could I? "That's fine, Joel." My tone was cautious. He stretched out to shake my hand, but all I offered was an uninspired look and an insipid wave.

"I've got a message from Obadiah for you. I was with him in his last day or two, with Yesh. Yesh's job was to bring you here."

"And what was yours?"

"Just the message. I had to tell you that you must speak to Sharon when you arrived."

That was harder than my heart as regards my sister. There was a temptation to turn on my heels and head back to my adopted home near Samaria, but three more days of sandy horizons and leg pain were more than I could bear.

I heard my voice telling him the terms and conditions. "So long as there's a neutral in the room, and that she's respectful. And doesn't expect wonders."

"Would Yesh and I do as referees?"

"I suppose so." I trusted Yesh.

Was a bridge mended? Maybe, it seemed temporary, at least. He left me to find my room, unpack and freshen up.

My wardrobe did me proud. In fact, I had rarely looked more presentable than I did that evening as I searched around for faces which I knew. Some were new, of course, and others known to me during the troubles. The leaders had a table together, raised on a stage. Obadiah's name was written on a sign above.

There was music. Joel was among the band, as songs of praise to the Lord were sung. There was joy and there was laughter. I did wonder how many hypocrites were among the assembled community, but the main speaker silenced my cynicism.

Obadiah, he said, knowing he was dying, had passed on the names of his network to Yesh, to be revealed and honoured once Jezebel was herself dead.

The time came sooner than anticipated, but the deed was done. He began at the beginning.

"When Obadiah saw the evil which was coming, he made preparations to keep the word of the Lord alive and unchanged in the unpredictability ahead. He recognised that the Lord had granted him influence in the palace, despite the wishes of the king and queen to accommodate Baal and other false gods in the culture of Israel.

As the experienced palace manager, he was also invaluable

to the smooth operation of every procedure and practice, a fact that was tacitly recognised by the royals. He was irreplaceable, despite his links with Elijah.

Yesh's late father was his first appointment, to be one of the palace guards. He had an ear to the ground for Obadiah, and a vital link in the chain. Later, Yesh himself became involved, firstly as Obadiah's servant and latterly, as his friend. To those two men, we owe much."

Yesh must have been the replacement on the day I took the traveller's message to Elijah's house. The jigsaw was starting to piece together.

"Next, we honour a man whose son has made a long journey to be with us."

I looked around. They were all staring at me.

"Eran's father was a faithful all along. Obadiah called him to the palace, and he was a regular visitor, carrying out his role overseeing palace security. Jezebel was led to believe that he was to work on and off site, listening for rumours, plots and plans in the city whilst keeping a tight rein on the guards."

So that's what he was doing, away from the farm all those times. But a faithful? They must have been misled.

Not so. The speaker continued. "He posed as the ultimate royalist, besotted by the queen and respectful of Ahab. That was a 24/7 role. No-one in Jezreel would have suspected he was anything but pro-terror, pro-crackdown, pro-Baal and pro-evil. His own wife didn't know, although she had occasional suspicions that he wasn't quite the man whom she'd married, or quite what he seemed."

Gobsmacked. No other word. How could I have missed that? I felt stupid. There was more.

"He lived a double life, totally committed to the faithful calling whilst manifesting as a dedicated, almost fanatical extremist."

I still didn't think any of them were very effective in their work. They didn't seem to have done much good in stopping the regime, but I listened on intently.

"He arranged with Obadiah that his elder child would apply to take up a vacancy in Jezebel's outer circle of make-up girls. She succeeded rather better than he'd hoped. As the years passed, her role was increasingly significant, eventually feeding Obadiah with up to the minute reports on the queen's thinking. Sharon became Jezebel's confidante, a two-way channel for Obadiah's instructions and her reactions. To her father, we have many reasons for thankfulness. And for Sharon, for her courage, calmness and coolness under extreme pressure, we have a major debt of gratitude."

Blow me away with a feather duster if you will, but what had they achieved? Grandad's torture was my starting point. There had been thousands of deaths and deportations, false gods gaining credence, sexual immorality encouraged under the badge of freedom, and most of all, the Lord being ignored.

Suddenly, it sunk in. Of course there had been clues. All Dad's business meetings while I worked the fields, the strange behaviours, the character change from the father I knew as a child, those unanswered questions which haunted me, those surreptitious winks between Dad and Sharon. He must have been in bits when his labourers were murdered. And I, spy-man, hadn't made the links. What an idiot. My sister must hate me.

The big crowd applauded vigorously, but for me, it wasn't

over. There was more for me to learn. Yesh's look was one of love as he put an arm around me, and I was led to where Joel was waiting. Remember the quiet nook off the city square? He was there, with Sharon.

She hugged me. I stood my ground, emotions all over the place, but couldn't put my arms around her. She backed off, disappointed, before speaking quietly. "Hello Eran. Joel has told me your side of the story, and I'm guessing that you know much of mine after this evening's event."

38

TWIST

I stayed tight-lipped. Joel glanced at her and decided to take up the narrative.

"I need to give you an explanation, Eran. I also had been given a role by Obadiah living a twin existence, like your dad had done earlier. Obadiah had identified me as a suitable candidate for his purposes from the time your father was employed to manage palace security. The house being opposite yours? That was not by chance."

I broke my self-imposed silence. "So, you mean my father knew all this?"

"Absolutely. That's why his antipathy towards me had to happen. It gave us both credibility. However, there was an unexpected twist which threw everything in the air."

"So, why did that scene in the palace play out as it did, Joel? Sharon reported her shock at seeing you."

"Let me explain the twist, Eran, and you'll understand. Sharon and I had fallen in love. Even Obadiah hadn't accounted for that one."

"And?"

"The chain of events sometimes left us out of communication. We both ad-libbed, if you like. We acted like it was over between us, but it never was. You just saw a scene with us both acting, that's all. I apologise that you were misled by Sharon's account, but the scenario we were in wasn't perfect. No-one could know, not even you. And there was other stuff which went awry, sometimes badly."

This was my chance. "Why did Grandad get tortured, Joel?" My voice was shaky. Sharon proffered her arm, but I pushed it away.

"Grandad? Your dad tried to stop him praising the Lord so loudly wherever he went. He told other people to be careful but didn't follow his own guidelines. He became overconfident. Don't blame Sharon. She didn't have the full picture then, just a partial understanding. Grandad's undoing was all his own responsibility. Sharon's influence was growing with Jezebel but was not as strong as it later became. She persuaded the queen not to have him killed. He got detained and tortured because that's what the system did to the outspoken faithfuls, usually before they were put to death. He knew the risk. Sharon and I loved him, as you did, and she did all she could. It hurt us both when he fell foul."

"Do you think Obadiah's resistance set-up was effective anywhere?" I was to the point.

"To understand the answer, you need to see this from the perspective of the Lord. He was showing mercy to those of His people who had turned away from Him, not just the royals. He was delaying punishment, thereby giving everyone time to repent. Obadiah was providing a source of hope through his network. A hope of better times ahead, a vision of an era when the Lord would have reclaimed His rightful place. That hope had to be based on facts, evidence, solid information from informed sources. We delivered that. So yes, as Elijah conveyed the Lord's tough love and justice in His words, Obadiah contributed to the mercy inherent in His delays."

"And you? How do you fit in?"

"Me? Firstly, I was taken into hiding by Obadiah when things kicked off, with ninety-nine other faithfuls. He fed and watered us all. But how did we pass the time?"

I had a guess. "Singing songs? Praying?"

"Some of the time, yes. Remember, the Lord works through His faithfuls. It's a team game. We also studied our history and our prophets. We prepared to be effective when restrictions eased. We were trained to strengthen the people in whatever circumstances we were in once their hearts softened. We were there to develop the hope which sprang from Obadiah's network."

"How did you find yourself at the palace in the first place, Joel? Take me back to what occurred prior to the scene with Sharon and Jezebel you've just explained."

"When my cover was nearly blown? Obadiah had picked me out for a vacancy on the palace grounds staff to back up Yesh's dad in his faithfuls' network, and the queen had seen me. She thought me handsome, I'm told. She gave orders that I was to serve her. For most employees, that meant one thing, that the queen was keen to involve you in her, erm, activity programme, if you follow me.

I couldn't warn Sharon, as it happened so fast. We had been seeing each other warily, as the circumstances allowed. Fortunately, we were both on the same wavelength, realising that one word getting out might destroy the network. So we flipped the story. We got away with it. The network survived, the people turned back to the Lord, and Elijah won."

I spotted the weakness in his account. "You referred to the fact that Jezebel liked what she saw when you were given the job. Surely to goodness, she didn't ignore a fine-looking specimen of muscular masculinity after a non-incident such as you have described?"

"Sharon was still having nightmares over the gruesome burials of the three young men in her early days for their refusal to take part in Jezebel's scenario. She had to act. After I had left their presence, she told the queen that, according to one or two of the make-up team girls, I was a waste of time in, erm, bedroom scenarios. She didn't bother me after that."

Sharon grinned. "It wasn't true, Eran. Come home with us. I have some people for you to meet."

I took her arm. Joel walked slightly ahead of us. I asked Sharon quietly if he was still writing worship songs.

"He is, Eran. You want to ask him to do his new one for you. It's inviting all the joyful and triumphant faithful to come together and celebrate God's victory. He doesn't think it will catch on, but I like it."

"Same instrument? God loves a good lyre."

She nodded knowingly. "Oldies but goldies, Eran. Mum told me that one. And Joel's been inspired by something further. It's about the faith shown by fathers who have gone before us. You might want to help him develop the theme."

I pursed my lips. "Can't do that. I'm not worthy, Shaz. No."

Just then, we came to the old family house. Joel turned to

me with a broad smile and pulled Shaz towards himself. Even I felt the love.

"Eran, my wife and I would like to welcome you home."

Relief, joy and tears cascaded through my whole being. In the kitchen were two teenagers, one a boy, the other a girl.

"Hi Mum. Hi Dad. And you must be Uncle Eran."

Sharon's grin was huge as she opened her arms to me. Joel and the youngsters joined us. I'd found my family.

"I've been a such a fool. A wretched idiot."

Joel squeezed my arm. "You are where you belong now, Eran, with your family. The banishment is over. None of us may understand the Lord's timing and His grace over the mighty events of our lifetime, but you know what? Let's celebrate His love, mercy, compassion and forgiveness at this moment of His bringing you back to us."

I managed a few words before my emotions got the better of me. "It was He who brought me home to you today. The Lord's timing is perfect. Let's worship this great God together. Joel, my friend, play for us."

Gratitude

I am once again indebted to a remarkable team of talented people who have supported me over the many months which the creation of this book has required.

Hilary Skinner has been an absolute rock in her work as principal editor, with invaluable assistance from Laurence and Jane Bozier, Rev. David Vestergaard, Mike Peacock and Dr. Phil Johnson.

Lucy Christian's thought-provoking artwork has added an extra dimension to the project, based on an original design idea from Amy Peacock.

Practical and logistical assistance has come courtesy of Dr Paul Cooke, Margi Lewis, Eirwyn Vaughan, Helen Stuart and Rev Jane Turner, with warm and ongoing encouragement from Lorna Dewhurst, Lorna Cockayne, Kevan Jones, Joanne Gately, Mike and Ann Shevlin, Caroline and Rachel Adamson, Rev. Roy Barton and Ben Field-Davies.